TH.

THE LAST LIES

A KATE MURPHY MYSTERY

C.C. JAMESON

The Last Lies

By C.C. Jameson

Thank you for taking the time to read this book. Please leave a review wherever you bought it or help spread the word by telling your friends about it. Thank you for your support.

Published by Creative Communication Solutions Ltd.

Last updated June 25th, 2018

Editing by Claire Taylor

———————

ISBN: 978-1-988639-33-8

Large Print ISBN: 978-1-988639-35-2

CONTENTS

Chapter 1   1

Chapter 2   14

Chapter 3   19

Chapter 4   36

Chapter 5   65

Chapter 6   78

Chapter 7   91

Chapter 8   105

Chapter 9   116

Chapter 10   138

Chapter 11   156

Chapter 12   165

Chapter 13   171

Excerpt from The Last Hope   176

About the Author   189

Author's Notes   191

Acknowledgments   195

To those who found the strength to speak up.
I'm proud of you.

CHAPTER ONE

A HIGH-PITCHED SQUEAL caught Officer Kate Murphy's attention.

Searching for the sound, she spotted an elderly woman in a well-tailored, baby-blue skirt and jacket pointing at a tall man sprinting away from her.

Kate rushed out of her patrol car and ran after the man fleeing with a large satchel under his arm. The baby-blue bag matched the senior woman's outfit—and it definitely didn't go with the man's dusty black hoody, jeans, and work boots. It wasn't hard to guess what had just happened.

Expertly zigzagging her way through the stop-and-go traffic, Kate shouted, "Boston Police!" over the bustling soundtrack of Washington Street and Dorchester Avenue.

Maintaining a fifty-yard lead on the sidewalk lined with various boutiques and cafes, the suspect turned to sneak a look at her. His towering frame stood out among the casually attired crowd meandering through the area, running errands, grabbing breakfast, or getting a late start to their workday.

Kate weaved around the pedestrians, heart racing and pounding. He had height, but she had speed, so she narrowed the distance between her and the suspect. In between breaths, her authoritative voice boomed, "Stop! Get on the ground!"

The suspect turned left on Dorchester Avenue, and Kate followed, further closing the gap between them.

A hundred feet.

Fifty feet.

Twenty feet.

Adrenaline rushed through Kate's veins. There was nothing like the thrill of catching someone in the act, righting wrongs. As she approached him, she gave it her all, her elbows pumping at her sides, her heartbeat echoing in her ears.

The suspect pushed a man in a business-suit out of his way before glancing back again. His eyes grew rounder when he spotted Kate right behind him.

But it was already too late.

She tackled him to the ground. Pinning him to the concrete sidewalk, she noticed a scar on his cheek partly hidden underneath two days of scruff. His jaw remained clenched while his chest heaved, expelling an overpowering aroma of onion. Up close like this, Kate guessed the man to be in his early twenties. She cuffed his wrists behind his back.

"That hurts!" he yelled.

She'd heard that before. A pathetic attempt at gaining sympathy. But she knew how to properly cuff, so he was fine. "You could have made it easier on yourself by stopping when I ordered you to," she said.

The man lifted his face to her. "I didn't do nothing."

"Is that so?" she asked, before patting him down where he lay. Kate retrieved his wallet from one of his jeans pockets.

"What are you doing? This is mine," he interjected.

"Don't worry. You'll get it back. I don't collect wallets."

Once satisfied with her search, she climbed off and pulled him to his feet.

He balanced himself just as the elderly woman whose bag he'd snatched reached them on the sidewalk. Kate finished searching his front. A pack of gum, shriveled receipts, and a pocket full of change. No knives or guns.

"Thank God you caught him!" the silver-haired woman said with an overly pronounced T.

British?

"May I have my purse back now?" she continued, her eyes darting toward it and its spilled contents on the sidewalk.

"Do you want to press charges, ma'am?"

The woman shook her head and pursed her wrinkled, peach-colored lips. A flicker of fear flashed through her gray eyes. "Dear God, no! I don't want to have to go to court."

"You probably wouldn't have to. I witnessed it as well. All you'd have to do right now is file a statement."

"Oh, I don't know, dear. This seems like an awful lot of work…"

"I get it. But this man's gonna do it again if you don't, and the police won't always be around to stop him—"

"I saw everything. I could provide a statement," someone with a low, hoarse voice said next to Kate.

She turned to look at the man with curly red hair. He seemed in his mid-twenties, dressed casually in jeans and a T-shirt.

"Great. Hang tight, sir," she said before reaching for the radio attached to her left shoulder.

"Harry-145. Requesting another unit to process statements for a robbery near the intersection of Washington Street and Dorchester Avenue," she said.

A few seconds later, the radio screeched with the dispatcher's voice to announce another unit was on its way.

Kate returned her attention to the woman. "What's your name, ma'am?"

"Elizabeth Greenwood."

"Okay. Please stay here, Ms. Greenwood," Kate said.

Keeping one hand on the suspect's elbow, Kate bent down to pick the woman's bag. The soft leather and heavy silver buckles made it obvious it was the real deal.

Handing it to Ms. Greenwood, Kate said, "I'll let you pick up your other items, then please go through your bag to make sure nothing's missing. I'll be back in a few minutes."

Kate walked around the corner, steering the suspect ahead of her, and crossed the street again, this time more carefully.

Once they reached her patrol car, parked next door to a coffee shop where she'd stopped to use the bathroom minutes earlier, she opened the backseat door to load him in.

"Watch your head," she said, placing her hand over his dusty brown hair to prevent him from hitting the frame and claiming police brutality.

As she closed the door, she spotted the other unit arriving and parking nearby.

When a tall and broad-shouldered officer walked out of the car, she tried not to roll her eyes at her bad luck.

Bower, argh. Out of them all, he's the one who shows up. Well, here's to nothing. She headed to meet him.

"What's going on, Murphy?" he asked as he approached.

"Suspect stole a woman's handbag," she said. "I caught him as he was running away. The woman is checking if anything's missing. I just need your help processing her statement and an additional witness's statement for the report while I take care of him."

He frowned. "She got her bag back?"

Kate nodded, and then she and her colleague headed across the street to where the small group of people was still gathered, including the elderly woman and the red-headed witness.

"So, is everything accounted for?" Kate asked the woman.

"Yes, thanks to you, Officer."

The woman dug a manicured hand into her newly returned bag, retrieving her wallet from which she pulled a crisp one-hundred-dollar bill that she offered to Kate. For a split second, images of the food Kate could buy, or the grateful smile on her uncle's face when she brought him groceries popped into her mind.

"Thank you, but I can't," Kate said. Taking payment as a reward was not only an offense she could get fired for, it also created too much of a slippery slope that led nowhere but down Dirty Cop Alley, out in Bribery Town. "This is Officer Bower, my colleague. He'll take your statement." Kate then faced the red-haired man before turning to Bower again. "And this man witnessed it all and would like to file a statement as well."

"Okay..." her colleague said, nodding and frowning.

"You both have a great day now," Kate said to the woman and the red-haired man. "I'll be processing the suspect in my car," she told Bower before crossing the street again.

Back in the driver's seat of her patrol car, she opened the man's wallet, sorting through it till she found his ID. Anthony Stefano Martolli. Twenty-two years old.

Kate entered his information into her computer. No outstanding warrants. No police involvement at all.

"New hobby I take it?" she said sarcastically to Martolli.

"Am I under arrest?"

"Yeah, let's make it official before I start asking you questions. You have the right to remain silent. Any statement

5

you make can and will be used against you in a court of law. You have the right to an attorney. If you can't afford an attorney, one will be provided for you. There. Happy now?"

"What are you arresting me for?"

"Stealing that woman's bag. What else, Mr. Martolli?"

Kate was halfway through writing Martolli's details in her official notepad when Bower knocked on her car window. She rolled it down.

"You can thank me now, Murphy. I got us out of filling those reports."

"What?"

"I convinced both the woman and the ginger kid that nothing needed to be filed. She got all of her belongings back, so she won't be pressing charges."

He's undone all my hard work?

Her shoulders tightened into knots, and her jaw clenched. She wanted to tell him he was wrong. She wanted to scream it at him. The kid would do it again if he got off scot-free. But she also knew from past experiences that arguing with Bower was pointless. And doing so right in front of a suspect in custody— though not for long, it seemed—was definitely not the place or time.

"Anyway. It's all sorted. You're welcome," Bower said before double-tapping on the roof of Kate's car.

"Does that mean I'm free to go?" Martolli asked from the backseat.

"Yep," Bower said as he opened the back door.

"Hold on, Bower," Kate said. "She may have dropped the charges, but I'm still recording this. I'm issuing him a ticket for disturbing the peace."

"Fuck! Here she goes again," Bower said.

Bower peeked in to make sure Martolli's foot wasn't in the

way before he closed the door. "You heard the lady," he said, then he stepped back to her window and lowered his voice a tad. "If paperwork gets you all wet, then suit yourself. My work here's done. I'm leaving. This report's all yours."

"Thanks, Bower," Kate said, the corners of her lips as high as her anger level.

She watched him return to his patrol car.

Bower's such an ass!

But being one of the most senior patrol officers as well as the tallest and biggest man in the district seemed to always get him his way. Who was she to get him to understand?

Martolli spoke up again, bringing her back to reality. "So, you'll let me go then?"

"Once I finish writing you this ticket, yes."

"That's it?"

"You'll have to show up in court. Probably walk away with a fine. But who knows? Not my call. You got off easy, so I hope you learned something from this."

Kate finished the ticket. With her paperwork ready and the man's ID back in his wallet, she once again exited her car, this time to release Martolli.

Once he was out of sight and she'd slipped back into the driver's seat, Kate let out a long breath to try to forget Bower's actions and his blatant disregard for proper protocol and regulations. The knots in her shoulders had started to loosen when, all of a sudden, an urge to empty her gut overtook her.

Damn it! Again?

She reached for the plastic grocery bag that held her lunch on the seat next to her. She flipped it, and, with a soft thud, her reusable containers landed on the passenger seat. She barely had time to bring the empty bag to her mouth before she threw up. Mostly liquid. For the third time this morning.

What's wrong with me?

She wiped her mouth and tucked a loose strand of blonde hair back into her ponytail.

I'm sooo glad this didn't happen while Bower was around.

As she breathed deeply, assessing whether the wave of nausea had passed, her phone beeped with a text message from her husband, Matt.

What's 4 dinner tonight?

Dinner? It's not even 10 a.m. yet!

Kate exhaled loudly, trying to calm her upset stomach and doing her best *not* to think about food while texting him back.

I haven't had a chance to think about it.

A second elapsed before his answer appeared on her phone.

I want lasagna.

She shook her head. The stench of bile in her bag was upsetting her stomach again, so she stepped out of her vehicle and walked to the nearest garbage bin to dispose of it.

Seated in her car again, she considered her dinner options. She wouldn't buy take-out like the last time he'd requested lasagna. That had resulted in a two-hour argument about savings and the various chemicals found in store-bought dishes. She'd have to make it for him. And Kate knew they didn't have all the ingredients at home either. *Argh.* Her shift ended at 4 p.m., and then she'd be stuck in traffic, and then the store... the long check-out lines... and then the time it'd take for her to prepare it...

But all those annoying details sure beat getting into yet another endless fight with her husband over something as silly as a meal.

Sure.

The Matt who'd cooked wonderfully and impressed her with his kitchen prowess when they'd started dating had disappeared since they'd gotten married two years ago.

Probably because he was busy being a great software salesman, traveling from lead to lead, turning them into six-figure clients. Yet, somehow, all those sales hadn't resulted in more income flowing into their bank account. That part didn't make sense to her. Why work late so many nights without getting paid for it?

But their anniversary was coming up in a few weeks, so she would give him the benefit of the doubt.

Who knows? Maybe he's planning to cook me a nice, romantic meal this year. Maybe he's been putting money aside, and he'll surprise me with a gift.

The sector radio crackled about a minor accident nearby, bringing her attention back to her job. If she wanted more money, she'd have to make it herself, and the best way to do that was a promotion to detective.

Best keep performing at work.

"Harry-145, I'm a few blocks away. Heading there now." She popped a breath mint then shifted the car into drive, pulling out onto Washington Street.

AT THE END of her shift, Kate returned to the station where

Julia, the newly appointed in-house psychologist, greeted her with a smile and another cup of her healthy, energy-boosting, antioxidant tea.

The redhead had somehow managed to create a full-time position for herself in some state-funded pilot program, and was constantly chit-chatting with police officers, like a butterfly going from badge to badge.

Does her task description include moral support or is it mostly mindless chatter?

But a light bulb came on in Kate's head.

Her tea! It could be what's making me sick!

Kate had downed two cups this morning before roll call. Maybe her stomach couldn't stand it.

With a smile and a quick excuse about being in a hurry to get home, Kate turned down Julia's tea then returned her patrol car keys before heading to her locker to change into her civilian clothes.

When she took off the T-shirt she wore underneath her uniform shirt, it dawned on her that she wouldn't have time to hit the gym or go for a run tonight, not with Matt's meal request. She shook her head at the thought and looked down, surprised to see her breasts spilling over the cups of her bra.

What the heck?

Bigger breasts were something she'd always wished for. But how? And why now? Did the Law of Attraction finally start working? Magically?

The nausea and swollen breasts certainly raised pregnancy flags, but it was impossible. She'd been on the pill for years. She wasn't ready to give up a job she loved to become a mom. At least not yet.

Not until she got over Bobby.

Bobby, her tiny baby brother.

Before she could take that risk with her heart, she needed to recover from the grisly memories of finding him dead in his crib more than fifteen years ago.

Flashes of that day still visited her here and there when she closed her eyes. It had happened so long ago—she was just a teenager back then—but who knew if she would ever move on?

But now's not the time to stroll down Reminiscence Lane back to my childhood.

Bigger tits or not, she had to change clothes and head home to please her husband.

Just as she was about to exit the locker room, she saw Johnston standing there, halfway blocking the door, his eyes glued to his smartphone.

"Have a good evening, Johnston," she said as she turned sideways to squeeze by him.

"Hey, Murphy. Did you hear?" he asked.

Kate stopped and turned to face him, surprised that he even bothered to talk to her. "Hear what?"

"Have a look," he said before offering his phone.

When Kate got a hold of it, Johnston pressed the play button to resume a video.

A few seconds into what seemed like random footage of a park and people's feet, Kate asked, "What am I looking at?"

"Dead pigeons. Let me rewind it for you."

Kate frowned. "What? What dead pigeons?"

"Not that I'd normally care about flying rats, but my son just sent me this video with dead pigeons he saw in McConnell Park. Weird shit, no? And who's to say how many got dragged away by cats, dogs, and whatever?"

"That's strange," Kate said, when she finally saw the part of the video that showed over a dozen pigeons lying on their sides. The positioning seemed random, as though the birds had fallen straight from the sky. Their legs stuck out like twigs from fat branches. Around them were breadcrumbs large enough to be visible on the shaky video.

"Yep, Anyway… They're pigeons. Guess they're not that exciting. Especially when dead. What are you up to? Fun plans for the evening?"

She raised her shoulders at the tall, husky blond man. Kate disliked small talk and preferred to keep her life private, especially since her colleagues didn't seem to care for her or Larson, the other female cop in the district. But she didn't want to sound impolite. "Nothing exciting. Heading home to cook dinner."

Johnston's shoulders slumped, and his eyes darkened, as though clouds had rolled in. "Gotta do what it takes to keep your home life working, right? Have a good one," he said before giving her a two-finger salute and leaving the entrance to walk toward his locker.

"You, too. See you tomorrow," Kate said.

She headed out of the building toward her Subaru, all the while wondering what he meant by his home-life comment.

As she unlocked her car door, she remembered: Johnston had lost an ugly custody battle a few months back and only got to see his son one weekend per month. That explained why he cared so much about the dumb video with dead pigeons. His son had sent it to him.

Cops were not known for their happy personal lives. She and Matt had certainly felt the pressure.

But the two of them had also shared adversities that very few people ever experienced. Kate had never met anyone else who understood what it was like to be orphaned. Her tragic childhood had forced her to develop a protective layer that no other man had managed to get through but Matt.

Matt's parents had died in a car accident. Drunk driver. With no older siblings or uncle to take him in, he had spent his teenage years being passed around from one foster home to another. That was just the destiny of most teenage orphan boys.

While the story of his parents' demise hadn't been as gory as Kate's, it had nonetheless left a scar on his soul. A scar so deep he was still going to therapy for it. Unfortunately, his therapist didn't accept insurance, so it added more financial stress to their household, but Kate understood the importance of such sessions for Matt's emotional well-being.

The fact that they shared such dark pasts had to count for something, right? Even with his grumpy flare-ups and his angry spurts, he was the only person she'd ever fallen in love with. The only man who'd managed to make her feel special. The only one—except for her uncle—who cared for her and made her feel normal.

But was their relationship strong enough to be the exception?

Or was it too late already?

CHAPTER TWO

————————

AT THE CRACK OF DAWN, Kate woke with an urgent need to vomit. She didn't bother to roll out of bed discreetly like she normally did; it would have been pointless considering the god-awful noise that echoed from the porcelain bowl seconds later.

"Shit," she muttered before wiping her mouth with the back of her hand.

That overly bubbly woman's healthy concoction can't still be in my system, can it? It's ridiculous!

Kate pushed herself up from the toilet and reached into the vanity where she kept her birth-control pills. She rotated the dial to today's tiny colored tablet before another wave of nausea hit, forcing her to whirl toward the toilet. In doing so, she banged the container against the edge of the counter, breaking loose the plastic cover and spilling the contents all over the floor.

"Shiiiiit…"

Once her urge to vomit had passed, she stared down at the pills scattered across the tiles.

Do I really want to pick these up and put them in my mouth later?

With the hours she'd been working lately, she had very little time to clean the apartment. Last time she'd mopped the floor would have been, what, two, three months ago? And Matt's urine always seemed to spray well past the toilet bowl.

I'll stop by the pharmacy and get new pills.

Another unplanned cost that would hurt her tiny budget. No way she'd take one of those dirty ones right now. She'd just have to take a double dose tomorrow morning. Thankfully, or not, sex had become an infrequent pastime, so the risk of getting pregnant from missing a single pill was likely nil.

"Are you okay?" Matt asked, his voice rough from the vestiges of sleep.

"Just puking my guts out," she grumbled, too low for him to hear. Then she spoke up to ease her husband's concerns, "I'm good. Sorry for the noise. Must be food poisoning or something."

"ONE MORE THING," Sergeant Bailey said near the end of his morning brief. "You may or may not have heard about this on TV or online, but there've been a few reports about dead pigeons and squirrels—"

"Who cares about those?" Bower heckled.

Kate caught Johnston's eye, and he shrugged. He appeared as surprised to hear this now as Kate was. He must not have been the one to mention it to their supervisor.

The sergeant exhaled loudly. "I know, Bower."

The room rumbled with annoyed grumbles and groans.

"Calm down, guys!" yelled the sergeant. "I get it. We've all got more important things to do—"

"*Much* more fucking important things, I'd say," Bower interjected.

"I know. Quiet, Bower. But the mayor cares, so we *have* to care. Or at least *pretend* to."

Another tremor of groans rumbled through the space as everyone around Kate shook their heads.

She did too after a few seconds.

After all, she understood how they all felt. Who cared about a few dead animals? She certainly didn't *want* them dead, but she'd joined the force to help *people* and to solve crimes. To restore justice and to put bad guys behind bars. Guys like those who'd murdered her family. She didn't join to protect the local wildlife—or pest, depending on how one saw pigeons and squirrels. Animals fell within other people's responsibilities, not the BPD's.

"I'm officially mentioning it here during my brief, so I can tell the district commander who will report back to the mayor and say that we'll *all* be on the lookout for any weirdo going around doing target practice on small animals… or poisoning them or whatever. The mayor doesn't want PETA, Greenpeace, or whatever animal-loving, tree-hugging organization talking shit about Boston, so that's his plan. Getting us involved."

Another wave of swear words, insults directed at the mayor, and other non-productive comments filled the room.

But Kate kept quiet.

As much as she wanted to fit in with the guys, she'd never been one to randomly insult people or disobey orders.

If that's what the mayor wants…

"Okay, enough!" yelled the sergeant. "What are you all still doing here? Get on with your duties, guys. Stay safe and keep your eyes open."

~

AFTER AN UNEVENTFUL SHIFT, while feeling a little freedom in her schedule since she hadn't received a special meal request from her husband today, Kate stopped by the drugstore to refill her prescription.

She mentally reviewed her upcoming bills and verified her checking account balance on her phone, and then she stepped into the store, happy to know she had enough to cover this unexpected expense without the risk of overdrafting or her card being rejected. A recent memory of that surfaced briefly.

Yeah… That was pretty embarrassing.

"Could you give me another three months' worth?" she asked the scrawny mustachioed pharmacist. "Can't believe I broke my last one this morning."

"You broke it?" he asked, his face scrunched up. "What do you mean?"

"I banged it, and it fell apart. My pills scattered everywhere."

He tilted his head slightly. "That's odd."

"Odd?" she repeated. "Goes with my unlucky streak, I guess."

The middle-aged man shrugged. "If you say so. Anything else?"

Kate shook her head, paid for her pills, and then walked out, puzzled. Before her mind started its downward spiral into random what-if theories, her gut churned, giving her a heads-up that she needed to find somewhere convenient to puke, and quick. She didn't have many options, so she settled on a young, sick-looking oak tree on the edge of the sidewalk.

Mostly clear liquid left Kate's throat and splattered on the dirt. Once she was certain her gut was done expelling its contents, she let go of the tree she'd recently nourished with her home-grown fertilizer, and then walked back to her car.

She had to make it home before Matt, so she could start preparing dinner for him and avoid getting into trouble.

CHAPTER THREE

AFTER YET ANOTHER SLEEPLESS NIGHT, Kate knew she had to top up her coffee mug to last the day. But Starbucks was definitely out of her budget.

So, coffee from the break room it was.

Free. Potent. Effective. Perfect for her current needs and financial constraints.

But when she walked in the room, she overheard Bower chatting with Andrews, one of their regular dispatchers. Ignoring the detailed and explicit description of his encounter with a large-breasted, blonde chick the previous night, Kate headed to the machine and filled her stainless-steel travel mug.

Why do men need to be so graphic about sex when they talk to each other?

There was enough of that in their mixed locker room, but now she had to overhear it in the break room as well?

She'd never been one to whine and bitch about feminism and stuff, but was human decency and respect for people's bodies too much to ask for in the workplace?

As though Bower had read her mind, he spoke louder, making Kate even more uncomfortable.

But Andrews seemed a little more decent than Bower.

"You should probably tone it down a bit," he said, nudging him with an elbow and nodding toward Kate.

"Pff. That's just Murphy. I'm not going to shut up on her behalf. She tried to create more work for me the other day. Hey, Murphy, you know that favor you owe me? I have an idea for how you can pay me back…"

Kate thought she knew where he was going with that and wasn't interested, not even a little. She didn't take the bait, and as soon as her travel mug was full, she hurried out of the break room.

Best get back to work if I want to impress my supervisor and make a difference in this world, however small it may be.

EVERY BOSTONIAN HAD FORGOTTEN how to drive—that was the only logical reason for fifteen accidents in the C-11 district alone. Exhausted, Kate returned her patrol car to the parking lot and was about to hit the locker room when the shift supervisor called after her.

"Murphy. Get in here."

Kate obeyed, wondering what she'd done wrong.

"Results from the detective's exam are in," he said as he stepped behind his desk and pointed to the chair in front of it for Kate to sit in.

"So?" she asked excitedly.

As soon as she sat down, a faint aroma of fish reached her nostrils. She swallowed her bile and made an effort to breathe through her mouth.

The supervisor read from a manila folder as he went on with his feedback. "You did well on the exam. Heck, you aced it. You beat the best score in the district, but... no, you're not ready. They didn't recommend you based on your file."

"What do you mean? You said it yourself. I aced the exam..."

"You're still young. Not mature enough. You need more experience under your belt, among other things."

What other things?

She took in a deep breath, mostly to absorb the somber news, but her inhalation included more fishiness than her stomach could stand.

"Excuse me," she said, rushing out of the office toward the bathroom. She couldn't make it all the way to the toilet; she tossed her cookies in the trashcan by the door. As soon as she was done, she splashed her face with cold water, swished out her mouth, and then left the bathroom.

Her supervisor was waiting right by the door as she exited.

Shit, he probably heard me puke.

"Murphy, what's going on?" he asked.

Kate shook her head, feeling heat rush to her cheeks. "I must have had a bad egg salad at lunch," she lied.

He eyed her up and down. "Is that so?" He squinted at her, arching an eyebrow.

Kate raised her shoulders. "Don't know. What else could it be?"

The sergeant shook his head, his lips pressed together. "And by the way, you may want to keep your thoughts to yourself."

"What do you mean, Sergeant?"

"Some of your shift mates were talking about you. Just so you know, nobody needs your advice on how to run things. Especially those who've been here for a decade longer than you.

If you want to stand a chance at becoming a detective, I recommend minding your own business."

Kate squeezed her fists and tightened her jaw before nodding and walking away, resisting the urge to find out who'd said such things.

No point. It was probably Bower.

KATE RETURNED to the locker room, packed her weapon in her portable locker box, took off her uniform shirt, and then headed home still wearing her boots, T-shirt, and work pants. Due to Matt's hatred toward firearms, she didn't normally take her weapons back to the apartment, but with an early-morning court appearance scheduled for tomorrow, it was much easier that way. Matt was just going to have to suck it up.

But her worries about being pregnant had taken over her life. Or at least all of her mental bandwidth.

This has to stop.

I have to find out for real.

I can't risk puking in front of the sergeant again.

With her weapon safely locked in the trunk of her Subaru, she stopped at Walmart on her way home to pick up a pregnancy test.

Kate walked into the store, found her way to the pharmacy section, and then stared at the selection.

Why are there so many brands? Are the pricier kits more accurate than the others? Nah. The cheaper ones should still work.

After two minutes of scanning and comparing, she settled on the pink box that included two sticks. It was on sale for $8.49. She figured she'd skip lunch once this week or 'forget' that Matt didn't like the no-name brand for a few items on their grocery list and that should make up for the extra expense in her budget. She bought the test and headed out of the busy store and back into her car.

Sitting at a red light twenty minutes away from her apartment, Kate realized she couldn't bring the pregnancy test home. There was no way she could deal with the results should they somehow—magically and inexplicably—be positive. And Kate was even less ready to talk about it with Matt. The kid issue had been settled a while back. When they'd first met, during one of their earlier dates, he'd mentioned that he wanted kids; she'd replied that she liked her career. They'd settled for 'Maybe later.' And that had been the end of the discussion. In two years of dating and nearly two more of married life, the subject had never resurfaced.

She pulled into a McDonald's lot and parked her car, breathing deep for courage. Then she grabbed the plastic bag containing the pregnancy test and made for the ladies' room. Inside the least gross of the two stalls, she opened the box and pulled out the roadmap-sized instruction pamphlet.

Several pages worth of legalese had been included along with the instructions. Kate skimmed her way through the sub-titles until she found the important part: wait five minutes.

Who wrote all this crap?

Seriously, all they needed to write was this:

1- pee on the stick; and
2- wait five minutes while praying to the deity of your choice or making a pact with the devil.

She only had enough pee in her for one shot, so she grabbed both sticks then set the box and its instructions aside. Armed with the two plastic widgets and a semi-full bladder,

Kate closed her eyes and let her hopes go down the toilet bowl along with her afternoon coffee.

Never did five minutes last so long.

Sitting in a public bathroom certainly didn't help either since it involved having her door banged on every thirty seconds or so by some impatient junk-food fanatic.

"Occupied!" Kate said for the umpteenth time.

The knocking was a good distraction, though. She didn't want to think about what she'd do if the tests gave her a positive result.

Or what if one stick turns out to be positive and the other negative? That'd involve spending more money on another test. Shit.

Mom and Dad, if you're up there looking at me now, please make those results—both of them—negative.

Kate shook her head.

Wishing for her dead parents to help her had never worked, but who knew? She needed all the help she could get.

She inhaled deeply, closed her eyes, and then exhaled.

"Here's to nothing," she whispered before holding up the sticks. Both showed the same: two vertical lines. The legend was printed next to the test areas, no need to check the instructions.

"Damn it!" she shouted.

"Hey? Everything okay?" a woman asked from the sink area.

Tears came up, but Kate pushed them back down. "I'm good," she replied before discarding the sticks, box, and accompanying literature in the garbage overflowing with stinky sanitary napkins.

She washed her hands, not daring to meet her own glance in the mirror.

How is this even possible?

She headed back to her car, lost in her thoughts.

She'd been good. She'd taken her pill every morning between 6:00 and 6:15. *Every freaking morning!* Except for this week, but she hadn't had sex with Matt recently. *How is this even possible?*

She unlocked her door and sat in the driver's seat. The pharmacist's expression haunted her for a brief second.

How breakable are these containers? Women were clumsy. Many were stashed in odd places and had probably seen much worse handling than how she'd inadvertently banged it this morning.

Did I get a bad batch of birth-control pills?

Could there have been a recall on them?

How the heck could I be pregnant?

Maybe it was a (double) false positive.

Could there be something in her system that would mimic the hormones the test was designed to detect? This sparked a sliver of hope in her heart. Google would know. She retrieved her phone but saw that it was already 5:25 p.m.

Shit. No time to look into this right now.

She had to get home, so she started her engine.

AS SHE'D FEARED, the slow-moving traffic caused Kate to arrive at the apartment after Matt, leaving her no time to research what she desperately wanted to know.

"Argh," Matt said, skipping any kind of cordial greeting as she walked through the door carrying her uniform and duty belt. "You brought your weapons home again?"

"Good evening to you, too, Matt. Hope you had a good day at work." She hung her belt in the closet and locked her gun in the safe.

When she closed the door to look his way, he was rolling his eyes at her.

"I don't do it to spite you, you know," Kate said. "I have an early court hearing. It's either that or me driving to the station and then back to court. Waste of gas. Waste of time."

"But I hate guns."

"We've been over this already. I only do it once or twice a month. Max. Come on. Give me a break. I'm exhausted."

"Who isn't? You think you're the only one who works all day?"

"I'm sorry, Matt."

"What's for dinner?"

"Give me a few minutes to shower, and then I'll make something, okay?"

"What I'd give to arrive to a home-cooked meal ready for me."

Kate decided to let that comment be. No point in arguing over who worked hardest. That was not the way to win an argument or save a marriage that was becoming rockier by the day. While Kate desperately needed to have a serious discussion with him and reestablish their boundaries, she was plain too exhausted—and too emotional—to open this can of worms right now.

Five minutes into her shower, the water was still cold. If it wasn't warm by now, that meant *someone* had already used it all up.

Matt's hair was wet, wasn't it?

He probably used it all up. Again.

She couldn't shake the feeling that this was an intentional move on Matt's part to get her to forego the shower and cook him dinner immediately. The thought made her seethe, so she pushed it aside. After all, she was only assuming. No point in getting herself worked up over nothing.

~

THEY ATE their pork chop and mashed potato dinner in silence, which Kate appreciated since it gave her the opportunity to think.

Matt spent most of his time texting someone on his phone, and the beeps of incoming messages were her only distractions from her pregnancy worries.

There just had to be an explanation.

Kate took out her phone and opened the browser to run a search but realized she didn't even know where to begin. She first needed to know the ingredients in Julia's healthy tea to determine whether it could mimic pregnancy hormones or not.

Or worse... Could the tea have decreased the efficacy of her birth-control pills?

Oh shit... Maybe that's what caused it.

Easy enough to find and confirm online once she'd asked Julia what was in it.

And Kate could potentially get the pills analyzed at the police lab to see if they contained abnormally low hormone levels—although using police resources for personal purposes would be difficult to pull off and definitely inappropriate. But it didn't matter anyway; she'd already put them in the garbage.

Then again, Matt probably hadn't emptied it.

He never did.

Kate pushed her chair back from the table, the legs of her seat screeching against the hard linoleum floor.

"Where are you going?" Matt asked. "You're not done eating."

27

Kate looked at her half-finished plate. "I have to pee," she lied.

"Can't it wait? Can't we just have dinner together in peace?"

Yeah. As though you haven't been ignoring me and focusing on whoever you're texting with?

But that was neither here nor there. Kate knew it was best to keep these thoughts to herself for now. She could just add it to her ever-expanding mental list of things that needed to change in their relationship.

"I should have gone before we sat down. Sorry, but I can't hold it anymore."

Matt exhaled loudly then shook his head at her. "Women and their tiny bladders."

Kate left the kitchen to go to the bathroom.

What an odd thing to say.

Kate closed the bathroom door and looked at the small garbage they kept by the toilet: an empty Target bag covered it. *Damn it!* Kate clenched her fists. Matt had taken the trouble to empty the garbage. Who would've thought?

And today of all days...

Now what?

She didn't need to pee, so she turned on the faucet to a trickle, just in case Matt could hear her. The last thing she wanted right now was to be caught in a lie, as innocuous as this one was.

Angry Matt's no fun.

The sound of the running faucet helped her concentrate. Her husband wasn't good with details. He could have missed something.

Heck, I could have missed one this morning when I tossed them in the trash.

Kate got down on her knees and inspected the floor. She lifted the plunger then the toilet brush. Nothing.

But then she saw a tiny yellow pill nudged against the back of the toilet's foot. She picked up her little dot of hope and placed it in the useless, tiny pocket of her jeans. Even if he went through her clothing before she had a chance to hide the pill at work, there was no way he'd find it there. As much as he was a control freak, he wasn't that detail oriented.

She flushed the toilet, just for show, then washed her hands, and returned to the kitchen.

"Feeling better?"

"Much, thanks." Kate smiled at her husband, who couldn't have looked more disinterested.

Their dollar-store cutlery clinked against their white Corelle plates as they continued eating. Kate stared at what was left of her meal, pushing a few peas toward her mashed potatoes. She didn't feel like eating anymore, so she gulped down some of her water while Matt stared at her.

Was he silently judging her for not finishing her plate?

"I'm going to save this for tomorrow's lunch," she finally said before standing up, plate in hands.

"As long as you don't throw it away."

"Don't worry. You know I don't waste food. We can't afford to."

"Damn right."

She walked a few steps to reach the counter and opened the cupboard where they kept their reusable plastic containers. "Did you ask your boss for a raise?"

"What? What are you talking about?" Matt snapped.

She turned to face him. "All of these great deals you're closing. I don't have a mind for business, but wouldn't it make sense to pay the sales team more when they perform well?

You're bringing them lots of business. Lots of money. Shouldn't they want you to keep up the good work by increasing your commission or something?"

"Get off my back, woman."

His glance froze her heart.

"Matt, could you please stop calling me 'woman'? I'm not a whore in a bar. I'm your freaking wife. I don't know what happened to 'baby,' but could you at least call me 'Kate' instead of 'woman'? I'm not stupid, and you know it. I work my ass off all day, and so do you. We don't splurge on anything. Look at this meal! Freaking canned veggies, bought on sale, meat that was marked fifty-percent off because it was starting to change color, and potatoes. How much more can we trim off from our expenses?"

"You could start by no longer donating money to your uncle."

"What?" Kate slammed her hands on the counter. "You know I don't give him much at all. I buy him some groceries and help with utilities when he can't quite make it. Am I supposed to let my only relative become homeless? Is that what you want me to do, Matt?"

"Are you menstruating again? Is this what this is about?"

"Fuck you, Matt. All I suggested was to ask your boss for a bit more money. You know I can't ask for a raise at work. I'm busting my ass, but I can't earn more unless I make detective. And I'm trying as hard as I can to do that. Just ain't happening."

"Simple. You should stay home and raise kids instead of putting your life at risk."

"What? And how the heck would we make ends meet? Less money coming in and an extra mouth to feed? Are you out of your freaking mind?"

He got up and walked over to the garbage can. His foot pushed open the lid, and he scraped a few bites of untouched pork into the garbage.

"Matt! What are you doing?"

He tossed his dish and cutlery in the sink before yelling, "What?"

"You're lecturing me on money and saving my leftovers while you're throwing away perfectly good meat?"

"I'll be eating out with clients tomorrow. I can't take a lunch bag to a restaurant. You know that."

"And what about *my* lunch? You could have just added your meat to it." Kate exhaled loudly as she pressed shut her container lid. She opened the fridge door and threw her leftovers next to a near-empty yogurt tub before addressing her husband again. "I'm going for a run to clear my head."

Matt left the kitchen and sat on the couch in front of his big-screen TV, remote in hand. "You're crazy. It's dark outside."

"I can't stay in this apartment one second longer," Kate said before heading to the bedroom to change into her workout clothes.

AS KATE'S feet pounded the pavement, thoughts bounced in her mind.

Am I going crazy? What's happening? What's my marriage turned into? When did we become that *couple? Where did the love disappear to?*

She checked for oncoming traffic before crossing the intersection.

Did he really bring up kids? Should I read something into his comment tonight? Could he have tampered with my pills?

Kate whizzed past a strolling couple holding hands, reminding her of better days in her relationship with Matt.

Is this all due to financial stress? Or am I imagining things worse than they are because of the test result? Could pregnancy hormones already be tinting my views on life?

Questions followed questions, but answers kept quiet, as though unwilling to participate in a debate that couldn't be won.

Or am I simply afraid of the real answers?

Just another question in an endless list.

First, she'd have to find out if there was a chance—any chance at all—that her test results were wrong.

A dog barked as she jogged past the bay window it guarded.

The steady thump of Kate's footsteps echoed in her ears, and beads of sweat rolled down her forehead. She wiped them off just as she spotted a man in a dark hoody a few yards ahead of her. After a quick check for cars, Kate crossed the street and continued jogging away from the lone man.

Chances were that she could outrun or beat the shit out of him or anyone who might try to attack her. But Kate knew from on-the-job experience that prevention was always best.

Matt had been right, though. It was dark, and their neighborhood wasn't the safest, even for a trained cop.

Why are so many streetlights off? I should really report those to the city, so they can be fixed.

A minute later, safely away from the hooded man, questions came back to haunt her.

And why do we have less money now than when I was living alone? Shouldn't two incomes and one apartment make things easier financially? After all, there's only one utility bill and one rent to pay. Fewer expenses overall…

Kate hadn't started to splurge.

That could only mean one thing. Matt had been splurging, but on what?

Did his therapist increase his rates again?

~

BY THE TIME she returned home, Matt was already in bed, snoring.

She had a quick shower—this time with the luxury of hot water—before putting on her PJs. She set her alarm for 5:30 a.m. then slid under the covers next to him. Though she tried to clear her mind, thoughts of her pregnancy floated atop her list of worries that wouldn't be tucked away for the night.

As sleep started to dim the edges of her conscious mind, breaking down the barriers she constructed to keep herself sane throughout the day, thoughts of the event she had spent so much time forgetting began to creep in.

Bobby.

Her baby brother.

She hadn't dreamed of him in such a long time, but there he was: his little brown eyes, his tiny hands. She remembered pushing him in his stroller whenever they went for a walk in their old neighborhood.

He'd been so small and delicate, but boy could he ever cry! Louder than a fire alarm. She had held him and rocked him to sleep when Mom would allow her to. She'd liked being responsible for someone else, and she'd loved him so much. She remembered the way he smelled; that weird baby smell that seemed to ooze out of every newborn. She recalled holding his milk bottle.

Ah… The first time she'd tried to feed him mashed carrots. Holy hell, he did not like those.

33

Most of them had ended up on the kitchen floor, the counters, the walls.

The kitchen walls…

In a flash, those same walls were painted with blood. She looked down at her arms and saw Baby Bobby, clutched against her teenage chest, his body cold and unresponsive.

She felt her heart break again.

"Bobby!" Kate yelped, sitting up in bed, drenched in sweat.

Matt stirred next to her. "Shut up! I'm trying to sleep."

Kate focused on steadying her shaky hands. She straightened her back and inhaled deeply.

Breathe in, 1-2-3-4. Breathe out, 1-2-3-4.

Bobby's dead. There's nothing I can do about it. Mom and Dad are dead. There's nothing I could have done to prevent it. I'm safe. I'm okay.

It wasn't her fault.

No, she couldn't blame herself for their murders while she was out of the house.

There was nothing I could have done to prevent it. She repeated that phrase in her mind once, twice, a dozen times, making it a temporary mantra, just like her psychiatrist had told her to do.

When her breathing finally returned to normal, Kate wiped her face with one hand.

Babies. They need constant protection. They can die if they're left alone. They're helpless little creatures. They need love. They need attention.

She looked at Matt lying next to her in their marital bed.

Would raising a baby with him help their relationship? Or would it be the straw that broke the back of their decrepit matrimonial camel?

She looked at the red numbers on her nightstand: 4:05 a.m.

There was no way she'd fall back asleep now, so she rolled out of bed and headed to the bathroom to take a shower and let her tears flow freely without worrying about Matt hearing her.

I'm not a teenager anymore. I'm a grown woman. Bobby died many, many years ago. I have to move on with my life. It doesn't matter anymore. If those tests are correct, I'll soon have a baby of my own... I have to get over my past.

Another sliver of hope formed in her mind.

Maybe her period would start tomorrow? But a few seconds of mental juggling made her remember the last time she'd had cramps. It was on her way back from work, after a particularly difficult day with a new officer shadowing her. That had been, what, almost two months ago?

Shit.

Another wave of tears overwhelmed her, and they joined the stream of hot water already running down the drain.

Kate had to accept it. She was pregnant.

Now what?

Could she keep it and get over the memories of Bobby?

There was another option, of course. But could she even consider it? Or would she have to ride this thing out, come hell or high water?

≈

CHAPTER FOUR

WHILE COURT APPEARANCES were part of Kate's duties, they certainly weren't her favorite way to start the day. But she loved the rest of the job, so she took them in stride.

"Officer Murphy, please relay what happened," the judge asked.

Using the facts she'd memorized from the photocopied documents minutes earlier, she began providing the details of the routine traffic stop.

When Kate paused for a second, the judge asked, "How long before Mr. Fartozi pulled over?"

"As I recall, it was until the first available spot appeared."

"Specifics, Officer Murphy?"

"Yes, Your Honor. Let me double-check my notes."

Out of habit, she reached for the notepad in her pocket and opened it, ignoring the photocopied documents in front of her.

That was when Kate realized something was wrong. Very wrong.

No matter how many times she flipped through the pages in

her official notebook, she couldn't find page 14. Her clip was on page 15. The one before said 13.

What the fuck? Who the heck had touched it? Who had ripped a page out of it?

"Sorry," Kate said, flipping back to page three. Thankfully, she didn't need the missing page right now. But she'd still have to figure out what had happened to it later and hope to hell that she never had to testify in court for whatever she'd noted down on it.

"The vehicle pulled over right after the intersection of Columbia and Devon Street, which is three street blocks from the speed trap location."

"Thank you, Officer Murphy. Please continue."

With the photocopies in front of her, Kate relayed the rest of the relevant facts and answered the judge's questions as he voiced them during her testimony.

"Do you have anything else to report?" he asked after all the pertinent details had been brought to court.

"No, Your Honor," Kate said.

"Thank you. You can return to your seat."

The judge asked Mr. Fartozi if he'd like to testify, but the short bald man rose and turned down his offer.

"Does Mr. Fartozi have other charges on his driving record?"

Kate stood up and shook her head. "Other than the unpaid parking tickets, I didn't find anything else in Mr. Fartozi's file."

Shortly thereafter, the judge issued a license suspension, fine, and a mandatory defensive driving program to Mr. Fartozi.

With Kate's court duties over and out of the way, she left the courthouse and returned to the station, puzzled as ever. She knew she had paperwork to complete, and she also had to get back out on the streets, but the missing page was top of mind.

Who'd had access to her notepad? Someone must have gone through her locker at work or her clothing at home. So, was it a co-worker or Matt? And why?

Who stood to gain anything from ripping a page out of her official notebook?

Sitting at a desk, as she flipped her pad open to page 15, she noticed very slight indents on it. Someone had written something—a string of numbers?—on page 14 before ripping it out. Kate had to find out what had been written there, so she grabbed a pencil and gently scratched the surface of page 15 with the lead.

Her own handwriting hadn't been pronounced enough to make out what she'd written, but whoever had jotted down the numbers had done so with more force.

It was a local phone number beginning with area code 617.

Without hesitation, Kate picked up the landline at the desk and dialed the number.

It rang. Once. Twice. Three times.

Then a nasally female voice picked up. "Good afternoon, Gisele's Salon. How may I help you?"

"Sorry, wrong number," Kate said before hanging up, even more bewildered than she'd been before. She proceeded to look up Gisele's Salon for its address.

Who would write a salon's number on my official pad and then rip the page off?

Sure, some of her co-workers were asses, but they knew not to mess with a legal document. And for a hair salon? There was only one other female cop and they barely ever crossed paths. No way she'd mess with Kate's notepad.

Her husband? Why the heck would he note down a salon's number? It's not like he had long hair that required services beyond what his regular barbershop could provide.

None of these options made sense.

Could the lady who picked up the phone be the blonde chick that Bower had bragged about banging a few days earlier?

Now, that would be the last straw.

～

KATE SPENT most of her days scoping out bathroom locations in between calls. She kept extra garbage bags in her car and extra tissues in her uniform. She also walked around with a nearly endless supply of strong, minty Halls and Tic Tacs, which helped with both her breath and her nausea. Her monthly budget was certainly going to suffer, but she'd make it work.

Thankfully, she was on dayshift, which meant she didn't have a partner due to budget cuts. More single patrol officers meant the district had doubled the number of cars that could be dispatched to answer calls. The increased vehicle maintenance was a tiny drop in the bucket compared to adding more officers to the payroll. She wasn't sure how she would have explained all the vomiting to a shift mate.

While she sometimes wished she had a partner, so Bower wouldn't be the other unit that showed up half the time, she had yet to encounter a situation for which she'd felt unprepared. And for that, she thanked the universe every day. She knew being a cop was inherently dangerous, but she was willing to live with that. If being a cop could help prevent violence and save other children from experiencing what she had seen as a teenager when her family was murdered, then it was all worth it.

Now that she knew why she was sick, she'd started paying

attention to which smells triggered her need to vomit: canned tuna and sardines, most perfumes, and, for some reason, freshly baked garlic bread. She'd also googled the heck out of morning sickness and found out that ginger ale and lollipops could help her stomach. (But sucking on the latter while in uniform was a big no-no, unfortunately.)

While manning yet another speed trap—this one near a shopping mall—she used her cellphone to research her abortion options. Knowing more about it should help her make an informed decision.

Massachusetts had legalized it, but it could only be done up to twenty-four weeks.

Why do pregnant people think in weeks instead of months like regular people?

She did the math: five and a half months. She still had time. She had no idea when the baby had been conceived, though. She and Matt typically had sex two times a week, though their sex life had changed over the past year. Long gone were their romantic evenings. And so was foreplay. Sex had become a mechanical act. She now understood why some people referred to making love as part of their *marital duties*.

All she knew was that she'd only missed one of her periods. The fetus wasn't older than eight weeks.

She'd probably have to see a doctor to determine the conception date. But the second she went to a doctor, she'd have to explain her absence either at work or at home, neither of which sounded good.

How the heck did this happen?

Kate was growing bored, waiting for a traffic violation to draw her out of her spot, when the dispatcher requested her current location and status.

A second after she reported her speed trap position, the

dispatcher spoke up again, "Harry-145, proceed to Ronan Park. Dead cat on the side of Mount Ida Road."

"I'm about ten minutes away. Heading over now."

As she made her way to the park, she pondered why it hadn't been an open call as per usual. And for a crappy dead cat?

Oh!

The dispatcher was Andrews, one of Bower's buddies. It all made sense now.

So not cool. Another one of Bower's practical jokes.

Last month he'd done the transparent plastic wrapper on the toilet seat. The month before that, he'd switched the salt and sugar in the break room. While those hadn't been aimed at her directly, she'd fallen for them.

But this one? It was personal. And all she'd done to upset him was do her job by the book. Following procedures—and rubbing Bower the wrong way—had landed her this crappy call.

Let's hope it's just the one.

Ronan Park was a nice, large park, and the silly call would give her a chance to breathe in some fresh air. There were much nicer green spaces in and around Boston, but Ronan wasn't the worst either, especially within Dorchester.

Right after parking her vehicle, she spotted a group of people who had gathered near the edge of the park on Mount Ida Road. They appeared to be chit-chatting among themselves, so Kate walked toward them.

"Officer! I'm the one who called," a chubby woman wearing yoga pants and a lime green T-shirt said loudly, waving her hand in the air as she jogged toward Kate. Her brown hair had been tied in a ponytail that bobbed up and down as she approached Kate.

"I found a dead cat," she said when she reached Kate. "A bunch of birds were pecking at it, but I don't think they're the ones who killed it. They certainly did a lot of damage, though. There's a hole in the poor cat."

"Did you call the municipality?" Kate asked.

"No, I called 9-1-1."

"For a dead cat?"

The woman frowned at Kate, apparently confused.

"Let's have a look," Kate said as she followed the woman's lead and headed toward the small group of people a hundred yards away.

"What's your name?" Kate asked on the walk over.

"Mariana Edwards."

As they reached the dead animal lying on a bed of gravel near a small landscaping wall, a slender brunette wearing nothing but black moved over to make room for Kate. In doing so, the goth brunette pushed a tall, scrawny blond man in overalls and bright red shoes out of their little circle. A young blond boy with a buzz cut and a faded-out superhero T-shirt was poking at an orange cat with a stick, a wide grin on his face.

"That's a dead cat indeed," Kate said while trying to ignore the disgusting scent and turning her attention back to the woman next to her. "Ms. Edwards, do you mind stepping aside with me?"

The woman nodded and followed Kate.

When they were out of earshot from the other people, Kate spoke up again.

"Listen. 9-1-1 is for emergencies. Real life-or-death situations, you know? If people start calling for things like dead animals, it'll clog the lines, and real emergencies won't be answered in time. Do you understand?"

"Oh. I'm sorry, Officer."

"Don't worry about it, but try not to do it again. Do you have a cellphone?"

The woman nodded at Kate, taking a black device out of her pocket.

"All you need to do is dial 3-1-1 and then report it. Someone at Animal Control will handle it."

"Okay, should I do that then?" the woman asked, her cheeks a little red.

"Like I said. No harm done this time. But please go ahead and call them now."

Kate could have easily called Animal Control herself, but she believed that citizens also had to do their part. They learned best by doing. If the woman called 3-1-1 this once, she'd be more likely to remember and do it later, if required.

Kate started walking away toward her patrol car as she overheard the woman reporting it via the proper channels. Kate pressed her radio button to update the dispatcher.

"Harry-145, stay on the scene. Pick up by Animal Control isn't sufficient. A full report is required," Andrews said.

Kate rolled her eyes. *Really?*

She could have sworn she heard Andrews giggle on the radio right before the static kicked in, but she knew better than to try to argue with the dispatcher.

Bower. This is his *idea.*

Here we go. Let the useless paperwork fest begin.

Kate walked back to the woman who had since put away her phone.

"I reported it; they're sending someone to pick it up. Should I do something else?" Ms. Edwards asked.

"Well… It appears this dead cat is more important than I

thought," Kate said. "I need to file a report on it, so I'd like to ask you a few questions if you don't mind."

"Not at all," she said, smiling.

"What time did you discover the dead cat?" Kate asked, retrieving her unofficial notepad from her left breast pocket. It was a similar shape and size to her other pad but didn't have the official page numbering. She knew her notes here would never make it to court, but she needed to write enough to fill out the official report at the end of her shift.

After thinking for a second or two, the woman spoke again. "About thirty minutes ago?"

Kate looked at her watch and made a note of the time. "And do you know or recognize the cat?"

"No, but there's a collar on it."

Kate lowered her notepad. "Let's have a look again, then."

When they reached the carcass, Kate resumed breathing through her mouth to avoid triggering nausea. The buzz-cut kid was still grinning as he played with the dead cat.

What's wrong with this boy? Why is he poking at it? Is he just bored and curious?

"Would you mind if I borrowed your stick?" Kate asked him.

The boy raised his shoulders and handed it to her before stepping away from the carcass.

Flies had already infested the wound. The feline was definitely dead. Kate squatted next to it and used the stick to move the collar, so she could flip the silver medal that hung off of it. She snapped a photo with her cellphone, hoping that she'd be able to read a phone number or something without having to touch it. She did have gloves on her belt but touching and moving a dead animal in her current situation was not appealing. The smell of it was making her queasy.

"Did anyone see what happened to this cat?" Kate asked the group.

She was met with shaking heads and quizzical expressions, and before she could ask a follow up question, the woman who'd reported the animal chimed in again.

"I walk through here every evening. It wasn't here last night at 9:30."

"Does anyone live around here?"

Ms. Edwards replied again, "I'm just a couple of blocks away from here."

"Did you hear anything suspicious? Gunshots? Animal fights?"

"We always hear cats in heat, but I think I heard a few dogs going crazy early this morning."

Kate looked up from her notepad. "And what time was that?"

"I was dead asleep. It was loud enough that it woke me up. My alarm clock said it was 5:35, so I went right back to sleep."

"Okay, thanks. Animal Control should be here shortly to remove the carcass. Please don't touch it. It's probably filled with germs and other nasty things you don't want to get on your hands."

Kate reflected on the 5:35 timing for a few seconds.

In this neighborhood? Too much time had gone by. It was late afternoon already. Stray dogs would have ripped this cat to pieces. *This has to have occurred more recently than that...*

A small pebble bounced near her boot. Then another, which hit the dead cat directly on the head.

The same boy who had been poking at the cat with the stick earlier had opted to throw small rocks at it instead.

Annoying as hell, but it wasn't like he was committing a crime.

But just as Kate was closing her notepad, another pebble hit her boot.

"Hey, young man. Could you please stop throwing pebbles at the carcass?"

That's just a preview of how I'll be as a mother. Argh.

As she finished speaking, one last pebble landed near her boot before he dropped the rest of his rocks.

The boy raised his shoulders and exhaled loudly, obviously annoyed at Kate for taking away all of his fun activities, one by one.

But when she looked down, she realized his last projectile wasn't gray like the others. It was a piece of shiny metal she was very familiar with.

She bent down and used the end of her long sleeve to grab the bullet. *Probably a twenty-two caliber.*

The head had been flattened by something more solid than the body of the cat near Kate's feet.

"Hey, kid!" she yelled at the boy, who was already ambling away toward another area of the park. "Where did you find this?" She held up the bullet.

He shrugged once more then pointed to a small stone wall that supported the slightly elevated landscape behind it.

Kate couldn't tell if there was any blood residue on it. If there were, it would be tainted by the boy's fingers anyway. Fingerprints would also be gone or well smudged, but maybe the bullet itself could prove useful. She pulled out a tissue from the tiny pack she carried and wrapped the bullet in it before placing it in her pocket.

Is this the bullet that killed the cat, or could it be from another crime?

She examined the cat again, stick in hand. The size of the hole where the flies were collecting in the matted-out fur made it plausible that the cat had been shot. But it wasn't like the department would ever approve funds to perform an autopsy on a cat to prove it.

Then again, the dispatcher had confirmed she had to file a report...

The possible weapon should be included in that report.

Shit.

Stupid Bower. Making me overthink a dead cat situation.

Kate walked over to where the boy had picked up the bullet. She traced an imaginary line from her foot to the cat, and then extended it to see where the shooter would have been positioned. For the bullet to hit the cat on the ground and then end up where she stood, it was obvious to Kate that the shooter hadn't been very high up. He would have most likely been lying in the grass somewhere farther back. There were lots of thick bushes around there. Or perhaps it was a stupid person, doing it right in the open. Or possibly shooting from the first or second floor of a home at the edge of the park on that street... In the distance, several trees stood, each with relatively low branches. Assuming someone shot the cat with a long-range weapon, the person could have been in one of those trees. It was summer, after all. Ronan Park had numerous trees filled with large, green leaves that could provide decent enough coverage.

But someone would have reported hearing a gunshot, right? Or our triangulation system would have picked it up.

Why am I even bothering with this?

It's just a stupid cat.

Unless the shooter hurt someone, and this bullet's just a stray bullet that happened to hit a very unlucky cat and then stop against the concrete here...

Or maybe the wacko's a serial killer working his way toward human kills.

He or she certainly wouldn't be the first... Numerous

examples of such a thing popped up in Kate's mind as she pondered that possibility.

Could it be why the dispatcher had instructed her to stay and file an actual report?

Could she have imagined Andrews's giggle?

She didn't know anymore, but she certainly knew better than to disobey an order, so she opened her unofficial notepad and sketched out the important elements: location of the dead cat, where the bullet was found (approximately), and the overall shape of the park. She then named the surrounding streets, so she could orient her sketch if needed later on.

After she was satisfied with her rough map—she'd recorded every possible detail her report would contain—she closed her notepad, returned it to her breast pocket, and then headed back to her patrol car to open the trunk. Searching through the tiny evidence kit she kept, she found a small plastic bag then dug out the tissue she'd placed in her pocket, dropping the bullet into the bag and sealing it as per protocol.

She closed her trunk just as Animal Control finally arrived.

Kate took in a deep breath and headed their way, passing a little girl on a tricycle, her mother next to her, shouting encouragement

Will that be me? Is this what my life could turn into?

The girl smiled at Kate as she passed her, her baby teeth spaced out in the front of her mouth.

Dentist fees for another person. And clothing. A baby would be a lot more than an extra mouth to feed. I would have to buy diapers, and lots of clothes as the kid outgrows them.

She hadn't bought any new outfits for herself in over a year.

How could they even afford to buy clothes and diapers for a kid? Hospital bills—

"Afternoon," said a short, tanned, curly-haired man in dark overalls as he opened the tailgate of his truck.

Kate snapped back to reality. "Good afternoon. Cat's all yours."

"Is that why you're here?" asked the man whose nametag read Jerry.

"A woman reported it using 9-1-1, and I was instructed to file a report about it. Crazy if you ask me," Kate said.

"Yep! But we've certainly picked up a *lot* of dead animals lately."

"And by a *lot* you mean…"

"I mean we're used to roadkill and the likes, but these past few weeks… I'm the supervisor at Animal Control, and I've had to hire two more guys just for these. Heck, I'm here doing pick-ups 'cause two ain't enough, but the city didn't approve more than that."

Kate let that sink in. She hadn't realized the problem was that widespread. The news had mentioned some of it, but not the full story. The frequency definitely explained why the mayor was upset, though.

"Can I ask if they're limited to one area of the city?" Kate asked as she followed Jerry to the orange tabby's carcass. He carried over a shovel and a black plastic bag.

"They're not in just one neighborhood. Before this one, I was up around Jamaica Pond to pick up dead ducks. Before that, I was at a golf club for dead pigeons."

"Today?"

"Yep," he said. "Since you're here, would you mind holding the bag open for me?"

"Of course," Kate said, doing her best not to inhale the nasty smell.

She brought the bag close to the fly-infested carcass, and,

with a grating sound, Jerry swiftly picked up the cat from the gravel area where it lay and then dropped it in the bag, stirring up flies, some of which grazed Kate's face.

As she flung one hand to push them away, she unintentionally wafted the odor toward her nose, which made her want to puke.

But she couldn't. Not right now. Not in front of Jerry, the Animal Control guy. Not in front of the small crowd that hadn't yet dissipated.

So, she did the only thing she could do. She swallowed her own puke back, but it didn't go unnoticed. At least not by Jerry.

"Okay there, Officer?" he asked, mocking her.

She smiled as best she could. "Can't say I'm a fan of the dead cat smell."

"I don't know anyone who is. Just be grateful it's not a dead skunk like the one I picked up yesterday."

A COUPLE OF HOURS LATER, after her shift officially ended, Kate made a brief stop by Gisele's Salon. She parked nearby then walked in front of the salon's large windows to scope out the scene. Kate spotted a young Asian woman with dozens of facial piercings behind the front desk. Around the receptionist worked not one but two busty bleached blondes: one was painting an elderly woman's roots, and the other was clipping away the tips of a young brunette's long strands.

One of them could be Bower's blonde one-night stand, but hair color and breast size didn't mean anything conclusive. Kate wasn't going to waltz in there and ask them if they'd recently slept with one of her colleagues—that would have been way too inappropriate, especially when she couldn't even think of a time when Bower would have had access to her notepad. So, Kate used the opportunity to walk into a nearby store and pick up Tic Tacs instead.

Purchase in hand, she headed back to the station where she once again ran into Julia and her Thermos.

"Officer Murphy, can I interest you in a cup of tea?"

"No, thank you, but I've been meaning to ask you. What's in it?"

"It's just a healthy blend of peppermint, Yerba mate, and South African red bush tea."

"Ah, thanks. Maybe tomorrow. Gotta run," she said before walking into the locker room.

From the second she stepped in, Kate's gut told her something was amiss.

First, it was Zhou that avoided eye contact when she gave him a head nod. Then, Johnston acted strange, too. He'd gradually increased his small talk toward her lately, but not today. He looked at the floor instead of greeting her. He closed his locker door and then walked right by her without looking at her.

The closer she got to her locker, the stronger her gut screamed something was wrong.

What's going on here?

And what's that smell?

"Hey, Murphy! Fun day today?" Bower asked with an overly happy tone as she got ahold of her lock and started entering her combination.

"What do you want?" Kate said, not at all amused as she concentrated on steadying her churning stomach.

Seriously, what's that smell?

"Heard you worked on a real important case."

"What do you mean?" she asked as she opened the locker,

releasing a potent dose of the bad aroma into the room, and making the half-dozen officers still present explode with laughter around her.

As Kate looked in, she recognized the matted orange fur resting at the bottom of her locker, flies buzzing around it.

"Fuck! Not cool, guys!" Before she could say anything else, her stomach reacted, so she ran to the large bin filled with used paper towels.

While she puked out her guts, a string of bad jokes and puns echoed around her. Most had to do with the dead cat, but some were aimed at her. She didn't catch them all, but the words "as dead as your career" and "desk duty where you belong" reached her ears.

Once she ascertained she was done puking, she unfolded her body from over the garbage can and wiped her mouth with the back of her hand.

"Bower. I know this was you. Fuck, man… You broke into my locker and planted the same dead cat you made me waste my time on? Forget about infringing on my privacy. Putting a fucking carcass in here is a health code violation! You better get that thing out of my locker now, or I'm reporting you."

"Come on, Murphy. Can't you take a joke?"

"That's no fucking joke. That's harassment!"

"Fuck you, Murphy. If you want to be part of the team, you gotta play along. I'm done helping you."

And with that, he left, taking along his buddies who continued to giggle under their breath. Zhou made fake puking noises at her as he walked by, pushing her toward her open locker.

And then the empty room fell silent, save for Kate's quiet sobs, which she managed to get under control within a minute or so.

Fucking Bower!

Since she'd joined the district, in addition to the various small pranks she'd fallen for, Kate had also heard tales of other officers receiving their official welcome by Bower and his friends. This tiny detail told her that the asshole hadn't played this particularly tasteless joke just because she was a woman, but...

And why do the rest of them always team up with him? They can't all be disrespectful assholes. Are they all afraid that not following his lead will land them on the receiving end of his pranks?

For fuck's sake, they're cops!

They should know right from wrong, no matter if the most senior patrol cop's the biggest bully on earth!

After wiping her tears, she called Animal Control and requested the carcass be picked up from the station. Then she found the janitor and begged for a garbage bag, so she could dump the carcass in there for now to reduce the nasty smell and confine the stupid flies.

Assessing which scenario would prove less damaging to her reputation and her likelihood of promotion, she decided against reporting Bower's shitty actions. While his pranks had no reason to exist in the workplace, she knew better. The police force was still mostly a man's game. Her supervisor was a guy's guy. He liked Bower. She didn't have real proof that he was the one who'd done it. She'd be creating a shitload of reports and paperwork.

And most importantly, Bower's payback would be intolerable. The man had no shame. And he had lots of friends on the force. She wasn't just fighting against him. He'd been working here for what, fifteen, twenty years? She'd have the entire district against her.

If getting the one shitty call for the cat today was an

indication, her career in this district could get a lot worse, and fast.

Kate had to admit it. She didn't fit in. *But fuck them. Fuck them all!*

Well, maybe not Johnston. Could he have been against the idea? Was this why he'd left the locker room before she became the laughing stock?

Can I just get one part of my life to work right now? One tiny fucking part? Is it too much to ask?

At least Bower and his stupid buddies will probably blame the carcass for my barfing.

She caressed her flat stomach and realized she wouldn't be able to keep it hidden for long. Her petite but strong figure would start showing at some point.

But for now, her secret was still safe, thanks to a stinky dead cat.

Talk about a shitty silver lining.

JERRY WAS the one who came for the dead cat. Again.

At first, he was confused, but he soon understood the crappy prank that had been played on Kate.

"I don't have time to deal with stupid jokes like these. I'll find out what fucker released that carcass to one of your officers instead of disposing of it, and I'll report it on my end. This," he said, lifting the bag and pointing to it, "is just not cool."

Feeling a little better from Jerry's parting comments, Kate showered and changed into her civilian clothes, which still stank of the dead cat, even though she'd aired them out while she showered.

She was just about to leave the station when her phone beeped.

A new text message from Matt had come in.

Your uncle called.

Is everything alright?

Don't know.
Call him.

Thanks.
Still at the station but heading home now.
Do you need me to pick anything up?

A minute passed without a response.

Screw it. I offered.

But then she hesitated. If Matt texted her while she was driving, and she missed it, he wouldn't be happy.

She decided to call Kenny now instead of later.

"Hey, Katie! How are you, darling?" he said as soon as he heard her voice.

"Great, how are you? Matt told me you called the house."

"Sure did. I just wanted to see if you're still coming over to play cards with me tonight."

"Of course. It's Tuesday! Why wouldn't I?"

"No, I figured you would, but"—he paused, swallowing hard enough for Kate to hear it—"I need your help again. Could you lend me a few dollars to cover my utility bill? It's due tomorrow. I know I ask a lot of you these days…"

Kate shook her head as she absorbed his request.

Where am I going to find extra money now?

"How much do you need?" she asked.

"I know I'm a burden on you. But their rates went up again. I can cover some of it, but I'm shy two hundred to cover the rest of my bills."

"Two hundred?!" Kate exclaimed.

He exhaled loudly on the phone. "I know. It's a lot. My health insurance didn't cover my pills this month. I had to pay for them upfront. Maybe they'll pay me back. I don't know."

"It's okay. It's okay," she repeated. "Don't worry about it. I'll... I'll find a way. See you in a few hours."

"Yes, and I can't wait to hear what you've been up to, Katie. You know how much you mean to me."

"I know. I'll see you tonight." She hung up.

Two hundred *dollars? Shit.*

She looked at her phone again to see if Matt had replied.

Finished the soap in the shower.
No more TP either.

She texted back.

I'll pick those up on my way home.

After stopping by Target, she crossed the road to her bank's ATM.

She entered her PIN, and then requested her balance on the screen.

$153.28.

Shit.

And it wasn't her latest $4 purchase that was to blame.

She retrieved $140 from her checking account since the machine only dispensed twenty-dollar bills.

Where the heck would she get the other $60 from?

Would Matt mind if she took it out of their joint savings account?

Better not do that.

They had agreed that their joint-account money would be used for a down payment on a house. That's why each of them put $200 per paycheck in there. They were approaching their two-year anniversary. One hundred and four weeks, so that would be... $20,800.

Wow. Hard to believe. But nice.

They may soon have enough for a down payment if they kept it up.

Kate tried to think of another way to get money. Maybe she had enough pocket change in that jar on her nightstand.

Probably.

But she knew she hadn't paid her Visa card yet, and her paycheck wouldn't arrive for another two days...

Fuck it. I'll deal with it then.

AFTER A QUICK AND mostly silent meal with Matt, Kate headed out the door with a bag of coins in her purse, dressed in leggings and a light sweatshirt.

Her uncle was at the door within a second of her ringing the bell. His thinning gray hair was neatly combed, and the ends of his thick mustache curled up when he greeted her.

"Katie! So glad to see you, come in!" he said, hugging her then clearing the way into the old home's entry hall.

Pictures of him with his wife, Lucy, when she was still

healthy covered the walls next to more pictures of her with a wig to cover her balding head after she'd begun her chemo treatments. A good portion of the portraits also featured Kate, after they'd adopted her.

She'd made happy memories here.

Funny how the years had gone by. The teenage girl she used to be had experienced horrible things, but Kenny and Lucy had made sure she'd grow up like a regular child. She had been loved and cherished. They'd done a great job. And thanks to them and her psychiatrist, she'd started to feel like a normal human and the feeling had stuck around. Well, most of the time, anyway.

"How have you been?" Kenny asked as they sat in the living room. "Here, put on a pair of slippers."

Kate recognized the brown and orange Phentex slippers Lucy loved to make and sat down to slide them on over her socks. While the old slippers weren't pretty, they were comfortable and reminded her of better times.

"Before I forget," Kate said, digging into her purse and taking out her wallet, "I'm really tight financially but here's what I could take out." She pulled out seven twenty-dollar bills from her wallet and then handed them over before returning to her purse to dig out a bag of coins. "And I think I've got about fifty dollars' worth here. Sorry, I couldn't scrape the extra ten dollars. Do you think it will be enough?"

Kenny hugged her again. "Thank you, Katie. This shouldn't be like this. I should be helping you, not the other way around. Your dad's probably looking down on me now and swearing, invoking our old Irish ancestors and cursing me."

"No, no! Stop that. You've taken such good care of me over the years. It's the least I can do, but I'm really sorry I couldn't find the other ten dollars. Matt's…"

Kenny pulled away and stared into her eyes. "What's going on with Matt?"

"We've been fighting over money a lot lately. I didn't want to make things worse and ask him if I could borrow a ten from him."

"What? That son of a bitch. He's not treating you right. You know that, don't ya?"

"He's… We're just going through a rough patch."

"Rough patch? You haven't looked happy in months. Are you sure it's just a rough patch?"

Kate raised her shoulders, eager to change topics. "Where's that deck of cards? I feel like kicking your ass."

Kenny squinted at her, making it clear her attempt at a diversion hadn't worked. But then he got up. "Can I get you something to drink? Decaf coffee?"

"Sure. That sounds nice."

Kenny headed to the kitchen and came back a few minutes later with two steaming mugs, a little sugar container, a tiny cup of milk, a tin box, and two spoons on a tray, which he rested on the coffee table. "And hold on a minute."

He looked into his old wooden buffet and came back with a bottle of Irish cream.

"You bought that?" Kate asked, taken aback.

"Don't be silly. The only booze I buy is crappy whiskey, but Maude, that pesky neighbor, brought it over a few evenings ago, along with a batch of these Rice Krispies Treats," he said, opening the tin box.

"Want some in your coffee?" he asked, holding up the bottle.

Kate shook her head. Although drinking would have been nice, she couldn't do it anymore. Not until she figured out if she was going to keep the baby.

"That's a first!" he said. "You're turning down booze? How about whiskey? It's probably the worst-tasting version you've ever come across, but it's the only one in my price range. I've been saving it for special occasions."

Kate shook her head again. "Plain coffee for me tonight, Kenny."

"Alright." He put away the bottles after pouring a bit of Irish cream into his mug.

"So, what are we playing?" he asked.

"Cribbage?"

"Sounds great." He opened the coffee table drawer and retrieved a wooden board and a well-used deck of cards decorated with a Florida sunset that matched her worn-out slippers.

After taking a seat on the old, faded chair next to the couch, Kenny shuffled the cards; his elderly fingers were still impressively agile, considering his age.

"How's your health? Everything good?" Kate asked.

"Of course. This old body's still got at least a decade in it, me thinks." He laughed as he motioned for her to cut the deck.

Kate did then reached for a Rice Krispies square. "These are good!" she exclaimed after biting into it.

"Unfortunately."

Kate frowned at her uncle, perplexed.

"Nosy Maude is annoying as hell, but she's a good cook. Can't resist her treats, but can't stand her."

Kate laughed.

"And I can't turn down free food," Kenny continued.

Kate laughed again. "We'll get our finances sorted out one day, I promise. When I make detective... That will help."

"About that. How's it going at work?"

Kate shook her head, mostly trying to forget about the day's events. While today had been particularly bad, it hadn't been the only time her colleagues had messed with her.

"I did well on the exam, but there's too much competition. Not enough openings. I'm keeping my eyes open and doing my best at work, but I'm not a brown-noser. Sometimes I feel like there's an invisible wall in front of me."

"Your time will come. I'm sure of it," he said, dealing the last cards, then asking Kate to cut again.

She did and Kenny flipped the card upwards: a four.

"Why did you and Lucy never have kids?" Kate asked out of the blue.

He paused, worry in his tired, brown eyes. "Now, that's an odd question to ask." Kenny discarded two cards and placed them face-down on the table.

Kate added her two discarded cards to the pile. "I was just wondering."

"You start. We thought about it before your parents…"

"But what?" Kate prompted after a few seconds of silence, blocking the memories of her family's murder as she played a card.

"You came into our lives and became our child, so there was no reason to consider having a child of our own."

"No reason? Or no financial room?"

"A bit of both, I guess." Kenny played a ten. "Twenty."

"Thirty," said Kate while adding a king.

Kenny shook his head. "Go."

"One for last." Kate moved her peg before returning her attention to her uncle.

He looked at her with crooked eyebrows. "Is something going on with you?" He played a king. "Ten."

"What do you mean?" Kate asked as she played a queen. "Twenty."

Kenny eyed his cards before opting for a six. "Twenty-six. You're hiding something from me. I know you. What's going on?"

"Nothing," Kate said, looking down and feeling her cheeks warm up. She brought her eyes back to her cards and played a five then moved her peg by two. "Two for thirty-one."

"Something's going on, all right... Dear Lord!" he exclaimed after a short pause. "No booze, baby question. Are you and Matt expecting?"

Kate froze.

"Is it that obvious?"

Kenny looked puzzled then smiled. "Oh, dear! Congratulations!" He leaned toward Kate then wrapped his arms around her.

She closed her eyes for a second before replying, her words muffled by his shoulder. "I'm not sure I'm happy about it."

"What do you mean?" Kenny let go of her and returned to his seat, his eyes locked onto Kate's.

"I was on the pill. I don't even understand how it's possible. I love my work, but I'll have to find something else to do. We can't afford to have a baby."

"Katie, you can't let finances be a deciding factor. We'll figure something out. You and Matt will figure something out. And I swear I'll find a way to help the two of you. Hell, maybe I'll get a job as one of those greeters at Walmart or something. Yeah... I could do that!"

"Don't be silly. You're not at an age where you should be spending hours standing up and walking around... But the thing is that I can't stop thinking about Baby Bobby." Tears started running down Kate's face.

A second later, Kenny was once again hugging her, his hands gently tapping her back. "There, there. Little Bobby's in a good place. Sure, his life was cut short, very short. But he had a happy existence. You can't let that affect your own life. You'd make a great mother, I know it."

Kate let her uncle's embrace comfort her for a minute or so before she pulled out of his arms.

"Thanks, Kenny."

He returned to his chair.

While doubts bounced in her head about his last statement, Kate looked at the cards on the table and noticed Kenny still had one to play. "Your turn, right?"

Kenny played his last card. "Four."

Kate shook her head. "I don't know. I really don't know."

Kenny moved his peg. "One for last. What's changed?"

"Matt and I. I'm not sure we're ready for a child."

"You haven't told him yet?"

"No. We've been fighting over everything and giving each other the silent treatment lately. I feel like I don't know him anymore. He's changed. Or maybe I've changed."

"It's normal. Lucy and I had our share of fights, believe you me!"

"Really? I never saw you two fight."

"Glad to hear. I'm sure Lucy's relieved to hear that as well," he said, looking up at the ceiling, kissing his fingers, and then crossing himself.

"I just don't know anymore. I might terminate the pregnancy."

"Oh no!" Kenny was now shaking his head so fast his hair couldn't keep up. "Anything but that."

"But—"

"Seriously. I know you don't agree with my religious views. I've never pushed them on you out of respect for your father. I knew him well enough to know he wanted you to choose your own faith. But I wonder if I've somehow failed you by not providing you with enough moral guidance."

"No, no. My moral compass is perfectly fine. You and Lucy have done a great job teaching me the difference between right and wrong. But maybe some people are not meant to be parents, you know?"

"Then maybe *adoption* is the answer. Not *abortion*." He paused for a while, his eyes never leaving hers. "Katie, please do me a favor. All I ask is that you think it through. Don't make a rash decision. Don't do anything you could regret for the rest of your life."

Kate exhaled loudly.

"And talk to Matt," Kenny continued. "He may be an ass—possibly the world's biggest—but he has the right to know. It's not just *your* baby."

CHAPTER FIVE

―――――

WHEN KATE WALKED into the room for the morning brief, she sensed something was amiss. Again.

But she didn't know what. She'd already had to deal with the dead cat. Did the guys crank it up a notch? Had they planned some other prank? And in front of the sergeant this time?

Why was everyone looking at her funny? Wasn't yesterday enough for them? Or were they just reliving it somehow?

She spotted Bower leaning toward Zhou, whispering something into his ear.

"Guys, have a seat. Let's get this over so you can start your day.

"First off, I obviously need to clarify things for some of you." He looked straight at Kate.

What did I do?

"I can't believe I'm about to say this. A couple of days ago, when I said to keep your eyes open for the whacko who's been killing animals, I was just mentioning it to cover my ass. And based on how you all reacted, I was pretty sure we were on the same page. I didn't expect any of you to take me seriously." He picked up a small evidence bag and lifted it up. In it was a single bullet. Her evidence bag.

Oh shit. Really?

"I'm *not* going to approve any ballistic testing on a bullet that killed a fucking cat. Stop wasting my time with this shit."

The eyes in the room turned toward Kate as a few officers laughed openly.

"Time to join Larson," Bower said.

A handful of officers chimed in. "Hear, hear."

No matter how much Kate wished the floor could open up and swallow her whole, it wasn't happening. She had no desire to leave her patrol duties and work a desk like the only other female officer in their district.

"To be fair, I didn't request a ballistic report. I bagged the bullet 'cause it was there in plain sight at the scene. And fuck it, guys. The dispatcher's the one who confirmed I had to file an official report."

The room rumbled again.

"Quiet, Murphy," Johnston whispered to her. "Keep talking, and your ass will end up on desk duty like Larson."

Kate knew Johnston was right, so she inhaled and bit her tongue while rage boiled in the pit of her stomach. Or was that morning sickness about to rear its head at the worst time?

Oh shit, it was.

Kate hurried out of the room and ran to the bathroom.

Great. Now the guys will think I'm a crybaby, she thought as she expelled the contents of her stomach into the porcelain.

A minute later, a Tic Tac in her mouth, she stepped back into the morning brief.

Johnston shook his head at her as she returned to her seat next to him.

"You shouldn't have left," he whispered.

Fuck. Don't I know it.

But exposing her morning sickness would also land her ass on desk duty. She was out of cards.

The morning brief ended with Sergeant Bailey calling out to Kate, "Murphy, in my office. Now!"

"WHAT'S GOING ON HERE? Did you leave the brief to go and cry in the bathroom?"

Fuck. Gotta lie your way out of this, Kate.

"No, Sergeant. You know I can take it. I'm one of the guys. But I... I had to puke. I must have had a bad burrito for breakfast."

Sergeant Bailey stared Kate down while stress-induced butterflies fluttered around in her stomach. "I believe you. Your breath smells like bile and Tic Tacs."

Kate's hand went up to cover her mouth. As if she hadn't been embarrassed enough already.

"But that doesn't explain your ridiculously detailed report about the dead cat."

"Sergeant, with all due respect, I only did what I thought I was asked to do. I'm sorry for misunderstanding your orders. Or maybe those relayed by the dispatcher."

The sergeant shook his head at Kate, his eyes showing nothing but resentment toward her.

"But remember Albert DeSalvo?" she added, knowing fair well she was walking on thin ice.

The sergeant walked around his desk and took a seat. "The

Boston Strangler? Of course! What BPD cop doesn't know his name?"

"Did you know that he started out with animals? I believe he shot arrows at dogs and cats, or some sort of animal torture, but the same holds true for many serial killers. What if we have a crazy person who's just getting started? What if these crimes are about to escalate?"

"Don't be ridiculous. It's probably a bunch of unsupervised kids going around playing bad pranks." Bailey grabbed his coffee mug and took a sip.

"I thought so, too. But the Animal Control supervisor I talked to when the dispatcher sent me to handle the dead cat made me realize how big the problem was. We're not talking about just a cat or two."

"Forget it, Murphy. Smile, nod, and keep the public and our mayor happy, but don't write up any more ridiculously detailed reports on animal deaths. Am I making myself clear?"

"Yes, Sergeant," Kate said after swallowing the knot in her throat.

She turned around and left his office as fast as her legs would let her.

Way to go, Kate. This certainly won't help your odds of making detective.

IN THE SAFE, solitary bubble of her patrol car, Kate reflected on her problems. While being bullied and having her official police notepad tampered with were bothering her greatly, her flailing home life and secret pregnancy took the top spots on her mental podium.

But other than her slightly bigger breasts, she could still hide her condition. She wasn't ready to tell anyone. First, she wanted to decide whether she would keep it. As long as she followed orders and didn't toss her cookies while at work, nobody would force her to get a desk job.

She remembered reading the memo about it a while back. Something to do with the department not being held responsible in the event a female officer miscarried at work. They couldn't legally fire someone for getting pregnant, but they could supposedly act in the woman's best interest and make her push paper at a desk until the little bugger came out and she recovered from the delivery.

Who wants to do that?

Patrolling wasn't always the most interesting job, but it at least gained her some experience toward the detective promotion she wanted. Filling out forms was not fun. It was already part of her regular duties, but in smaller doses. She didn't want it to become a full-time job.

But what about telling Matt?

She knew Kenny was right. Matt deserved to know, but she wasn't ready to tell him yet. She still had to figure out how the pregnancy had happened in the first place.

Earlier that morning, she googled the psychologist's tea ingredients, but found no indication they could have weakened her birth-control pills. She also googled her particular brand of contraceptives and there hadn't been any recall. They were 99.99% reliable. No way she was the 0.01% statistics in this. Someone had to have tampered with her pills.

As much as she hated Bower and suspected he was the one who'd orchestrated the dead cat prank and possibly ripped a page out of her notepad, she couldn't come up with one scenario where he would have had access to her pills. While he obviously knew her locker combination and could have accessed her notepad in there, Kate had never taken her pills to work. She'd always kept them in the privacy of her apartment bathroom.

Bower had never been to her place.

So, the only option was Matt. *But why?*

Why—*and how*—would he have tampered with her pills?

She didn't know how to answer this question. Kate still had the pill she'd found on the floor, but she didn't have a friend at the lab. She didn't have many friends at all if she were honest with herself. She couldn't use the department's resources, and she wasn't going to cheat the system either. She could probably find a lab that could test the pill for her, but it would cost money, money she didn't have.

After writing a handful of speeding tickets and responding to a robbery, she headed back to the station with lots of reports to file. It was unlikely the robbery victim would ever get his electronics back, but who knew? The only thing she could really do was her work: file the report and maybe one day, the stolen items would appear in a warehouse or turn up at a pawn shop.

Unlikely, but possible.

Just like Matt tampering with her pills.

Unlikely, but possible.

Unfortunately, it changed nothing to the fact that a fetus was growing inside of her.

The clock was ticking.

Not only did she have to make up her mind about what she'd do with it, but she also had to tell Matt. Announcing the news to her husband could no longer wait.

She would do it tonight.

KATE ARRIVED HOME WELL past sunset.

"Matt? Babe?" she said after unlocking the front door.

No answer, but the sound of a running shower reached her ears.

She walked through the bedroom and popped her head in the bathroom.

"I'm back!" she yelled over the noise of the running water.

"I'll be out in a few minutes," Matt replied.

I've got some time to figure this out.

She sat on their marital bed, the very place where this new life had probably been conceived. It wasn't as though they'd had sex in many other places recently. They used to be all over each other anywhere and everywhere. Now, because they were rarely in bed and awake at the same time, they were lucky if it happened twice a week.

"Matt, I'm pregnant," she rehearsed aloud.

That's awful. You can do better than that!

"Matt, sit down, I've got something to tell you."

Better. But then what?

They say a picture is worth a thousand words. Maybe I can show him with a picture. That's an idea...

Kate had never been a good artist. She couldn't draw anything more complex than a stick figure. She looked around the room and spotted Matt's phone on his nightstand.

I can change his phone background to a baby picture!

Although she'd never accessed his phone without his permission before, she knew his password. She kept nagging him about the importance of using complex passwords and changing them regularly, but he used the same one for everything.

She unlocked her husband's mobile screen then opened the browser to look for a baby picture online. She found one that showed a baby with a "Congrats, you'll be a dad!" sign on it.

Good enough.

She had just pressed save to make it his new screensaver when a text message came in.

We gotta do this again.

The sender's name was Sam.

Normally Kate wouldn't have thought anything about it, probably someone he'd done business with, but the little picture that accompanied the message was of a woman's cleavage.

Who freaking uses a thumbnail of their breasts as a profile pic?

Curious—or maybe the pregnancy hormones were clouding her judgment—Kate clicked on the thumbnail to see Sam's contact information. A larger version of the woman's huge breasts appeared.

What the heck?

She felt the urge to read the previous messages they'd exchanged, but at the same time, she didn't want to know.

Kate marked the message as unread and dropped the phone where he'd left it before trading her work clothes for running gear and then heading out the door just as the shower shut off.

AS HER FEET hit the pavement and her breathing settled into a comfortable rhythm, her thoughts kept tumbling around in her head.

There was no incriminating evidence.

She didn't have proof of anything. Sam could be a woman he'd had a business meeting with and that was all.

But why the shower after a business dinner?

Stop being suspicious, Kate. It's your husband.

She crossed the street and continued running on the sidewalk, once again noting the streetlights that weren't working.

I really need to report those.

But she didn't have her phone right now. She'd do it when she got home.

Shit, did I save the image or not?

Kate was pretty sure she had.

Shit.

Matt would have seen it by now, and he'd probably tried to call her. He might be worried sick. His pregnant wife had yet again gone out running in the dark by herself.

I'll head back home and see how he reacts.

Will he act guilty? Will he blame me? Or will he be happy?

His reaction would tell her all she needed to know.

"BABY! You had me worried! Where did you go?" Matt asked when Kate walked through the door.

He jumped up from the couch and ran toward her, hugging her sweaty body. "We're going to have a baby! You've made me so happy! But why did you leave me that image on my phone and then leave the house? You don't know what I've been through this past half-hour. I... I couldn't figure out where you'd gone. Why you'd left the house. Are you alright?"

"I just wanted to get my exercise in. You know me."

"Oh, is that all? I was worried."

"What were you worried about?" Kate asked.

"Don't get me started. You know I hate it when you go out running alone at night. And now you have a little us inside of you. You can't be doing that anymore. And you'll have to quit your job. It's not good for the baby."

"Matt, hold your horses." She held his hand and walked him back to the couch. She turned off the basketball game that played in the background. "I apologize, I shouldn't have left you that photo then ran out the door. But I think we need to talk. If we're going to have a baby, we need to be clear about our roles and how things will change... or not."

"Certainly, baby. We'll make this work," he said, gripping her hands then pulling away when his phone beeped. He got up and headed to the kitchen, taking out the phone as he did. "Want something to eat now? How about I re-heat some of that chili you made? Wouldn't that be great?"

"Sure. That sounds good," Kate said, wishing she was a little bird so she could have a look at his phone right now. Was it another message from Sam?

Matt was being really nice to her right now, suspiciously so. Like back when they'd started dating. *That* Matt hadn't made an appearance in a very long time.

A shiver ran up her spine.

I have to get out of my sweaty clothes.

"Actually, Matt, could you hold off on re-heating my chili? I want to take a shower first." She peeked her head into the kitchen.

Her husband's face was glued to his phone. He barely acknowledged her request with an "Uh-huh."

Kate made her way to the bathroom and let the lukewarm

water soothe her worries. Even though she tried, she couldn't shake the feeling that something was up. Matt had acted so... weird. He'd been nice and caring, of course, but strangely so. Like the Matt she'd met years ago when they both used to volunteer at the food bank, when she fell in love with him.

The thoughtful gestures, the four-course meals, the flowers for no reason, the relaxing massages he used to give her. But even as the good memories from the beginning of their relationship filled her mind, Kate couldn't help but think he was up to no-good with that Sam.

Could Sam be the reason he was so happy? Or maybe he saw this pregnancy as a way to have a family again...

Yeah. That made sense. The orphan in him would be getting a new family. It would be awesome for him.

But unlike Kate, he hadn't lost a sibling when he'd become orphaned. He had no negative associations with babies.

While her thoughts bounced around, what was left of the warm water disappeared, so Kate stepped out of the shower, grabbed her towel from above the toilet, and then patted herself dry.

She wiped the light layer of condensation off of the mirror and stared at her reflection. She moved her hand across her flat stomach, not feeling anything different, then opened the door. The smell of chili waltzed into the bathroom, and she wrapped herself in her towel before stepping into their bedroom to put on her pajamas.

When she entered the kitchen, Matt was nowhere to be found but had left the pot of chili on the stovetop. She popped open the lid. It was empty, save for a tablespoon worth if she were to scrape it all off.

"Did you save me some?"

Matt didn't answer. The sound of the basketball game was apparently more important than Kate's words.

She poked her head in the living room, where Matt sat on the couch. "Did you save me some chili?"

"What? No. There wasn't enough for two, sorry."

Her blood boiled in her veins.

"Damn it, Matt. This shit has to stop! First, you offer me some, and then you tell me it's all gone? This is a fucking dick move! Why is it that *your* needs always come first? What about *my* needs? What about caring about me, about what I want for a change?"

"Get over it, it was just chili," he said, tossing his hand at Kate's remarks.

She marched over to the TV and pressed the power button.

"Hey! Turn it back on!" he ordered.

"No. Not until you acknowledge that you have to treat me better. I'm your wife, Matt. Not just some tramp you met in a bar. I think we need to go see someone. A professional. Get help with our relationship."

"Whatever. Turn the TV back on, woman."

"That's another thing. We need to cancel the cable plan. We can't afford it, Matt. I'm tired of having to scrape every penny to find enough money for us to eat. We can't afford cable."

"Life without TV is no life at all. Not going to happen."

Kate inhaled deeply. "You're such a selfish ass!" She wanted to expand her list of insults but stopped herself before saying something she knew she would regret later. Matt had never turned to physical violence, but deep down she sensed he was capable of it. She spun her wedding ring on her finger, and exhaled loudly, diffusing some of her anger.

She returned to the kitchen, opened the fridge to see what

she could put together to eat, but some smell wafting from inside turned her stomach.

She rushed to the bathroom to empty her gut, yet again.

Would raising a baby with Matt make sense? If their relationship didn't change, the eighteen years to come were going to be very, very long.

CHAPTER SIX

BEFORE SHE'D LEFT for work, Matt had crawled out of bed to kiss her goodbye. His abnormally warm behavior left her puzzled during her morning commute to the precinct.

But her focus shifted when she spotted a Post-It Note on her locker. It read: "Murphy, Sergeant's office ASAP."

Fuck. Again? What now?

The second she was dressed in her uniform, she headed to meet him. As though he'd been waiting for her, he'd left his office door opened.

Kate knocked on the doorframe. "Sergeant? You wanted to see me?"

"Murphy, yes. Come in. Take a seat," he said, standing and pointing to the chair in front of his desk before closing his door and returning to his seat.

The air was heavy with something Kate couldn't identify, and a deep wrinkle bisected Sergeant Bailey's dark eyebrows.

He finally broke the silence and waved a piece of paper over his desk, in the air between them.

"I just heard. Is it true?"

"I'm not sure. What are you talking about, Sergeant?" asked Kate.

"Some Jerry Swanson guy emailed me this morning."

Kate frowned, trying to remember who that was.

"Let me give you another hint. He works with Animal Control."

Oh no. *That* Jerry. Shit. Kate couldn't look at the sergeant.

"Based on your reaction, I take it it's true. Was it Bower?"

Kate swallowed hard, her eyes still on the concrete floor.

How do I act now?

"Murphy, look at me."

Kate did, even though she could feel her eyes tearing up, which was the last thing she wanted her supervisor to see. Through her moist eyes, she saw the sergeant's traits soften and the corner of his lips rise.

Wait, is he siding with me on this?

"Why didn't you report it to me?" he asked.

Kate brought a finger to her nose, scratching it, although it didn't itch. But it was something to distract her, to help her contain her tears.

"Why?" she repeated before inhaling deeply.

"Murphy…"

Her distraction tactic hadn't worked. *Stupid pregnancy hormones. Are they making me more emotional than usual?* She wiped a tear from her eye before it flowed down her cheek. "Contrary to what it looks like right now, I'm not a crybaby, Sergeant."

"I've never called you one. I may have asked about—"

"I'm a team player. I know I make mistakes sometimes. But I love being a police officer. There's nothing I want more in the world than to become a detective. I know the job comes with its fair share of bullsh—" Kate interrupted herself. "Sorry, Sergeant. I don't mean—"

"Murphy. I don't care whether you're a woman or a man. I realize the guys probably make your life a little hard at times. Boys will be boys and all. But that..." He waved the printed email in the air again. "It's too much. You should have reported it to me the minute it happened. This shouldn't be the way I hear about it."

A blast of hope blew past Kate's heart, causing tears to spill from her eyes.

"I'm sorry, Sergeant. I... I just didn't want to make things worse for myself."

"You know who did it?" the sergeant asked.

"I have an idea, but no proof. So, I won't say."

"I'm not blind. I know who you suspect. I'll deal with him. But I want one thing to be crystal clear. This type of behavior, this..." He tapped his finger on the printed email again. "This is not acceptable. I will not tolerate this kind of behavior. And this goes for *all* my officers. I'm not treating you any differently. It may not have been your *fault*, but it's *your responsibility* to report it to me if it happens again. This kind of shit won't fly here."

"Yes, Sergeant."

"I'm heading out for coffee." He stood up and reached behind him to grab a box of tissues, which he offered to Kate. "Pull yourself together, and then close my office door after you leave."

After a couple of minutes of deep inhaling and exhaling, Kate managed to dry her eyes and prep herself for the day.

Backlash was coming for certain.

Bower would never be the kind to receive criticism from the sergeant without trashing Kate in return. And the district included too many of Bower's friends and allies.

But at least she knew she hadn't been the one to report him. He couldn't accuse her of that, and that was a small comfort. So, with her newly talked-into confidence, she got up from her chair, left the sergeant's office, and closed the door on her way out.

~

"OPERATIONS TO HARRY-145," the dispatcher said on the radio.

Kate replied right away. "Harry-145."

"80 Neponset Avenue, disturbance."

"Harry-145 acknowledged."

She ran lights and sirens to the address provided for the call. As she arrived, she saw a sign that said *Exotic Pet Frenzy*.

"Harry-145. Adam Robert," Kate said on the radio to announce her arrival at the scene.

The dispatcher acknowledged her statement, and Kate exited her vehicle.

She noticed a *Help Wanted* sign as she opened the door. A bell rang just above it as she entered, but it barely registered above the sound of the feuding men behind the counter at the back of the store.

A mother stood with her hands over her young daughter's ears. The daughter's eyes were round, and the mother was shaking her head.

Kate jabbed a thumb toward the door, instructing the mother and child to go wait outside.

They obeyed, leaving their basket in the aisle.

Why is it that some people don't just walk away? Wouldn't it have been easier to leave the premises instead of just covering your child's ears?

Then Kate reflected on her judgment of that woman.

Who knew? Kate herself could end up being the worst mom ever. She shouldn't judge any mother.

But she tossed that negative thought aside for now and continued to the back of the store, keeping an eye out for other civilians. But from what she could tell, she and the two arguing men in matching green aprons were the only ones left.

As she approached the counter, she paid close attention to the two Caucasian males behind it. The man on the left, closest to the cash register, was around five feet seven, his hair gray, with a thick, matching mustache decorating his upper lip. Probably in his early fifties. The one on the right was six-feet tall, blond, scrawny, and most likely in his early- or mid-twenties. Something about him seemed familiar. Kate wondered if she'd seen him in the grocery store or issued him a speeding ticket recently.

"Okay, okay! Stop it now!" Kate yelled as she reached the counter, her authoritative voice booming as loud as theirs. The older man shut up and turned to face her while the young one continued hollering.

Kate slapped her hand on the counter next to the young man. "Sir, please stop yelling."

As though snapping out of a trance, the man stopped and slowly turned to look at Kate.

"I'm Officer Murphy. Someone reported a disturbance. That's why I'm—"

The young man resumed yelling at the older man, who returned the shouting. The only words Kate made out were "thief," "overtime," "fired," and "missing inventory."

Kate slammed her hand on the counter again. "Enough!"

The two men shut up. This time for real.

Kate lowered her voice to a near whisper. "Listen, and don't you dare start yelling again. This is how it's going to work.

Either you behave and listen to me, or I'm taking you both in right now."

The older man nodded while the young man remained silent and motionless, which Kate took as a sign of comprehension.

She retrieved her official notepad. Turning to the obedient, older man, she asked, "Sir, what's your name?"

"Thomas Tumlinson," he said.

"And do you work here?"

"I own this pet shop. So, yes, I work here."

"Can I see some ID, please?"

The man pulled his wallet out of his pants, then retrieved his driver's license and handed it to Kate who copied down his information.

"Thank you," Kate said.

She turned to the other man. "And you, sir? What's your name?"

"Frank Scott," he said, his voice flat.

"ID?"

The man provided it.

As she returned the driver's license to the young man, she knew her next question could trigger another yelling spree based on what she'd already overheard between them, so she prefaced it with, "Now, don't start arguing over this next bit. You'll both get a chance to answer questions. One at a time, all right?"

She once again glared at both men, who now both nodded in agreement.

"Mr. Scott, do you work here?" Kate asked.

"Yes, I—"

"Officer," the owner interrupted.

Kate turned to the owner. "As I said, I'll give you a chance to speak in a second. Let me hear his story. Then I'll ask you the same questions."

The owner's cheeks reddened, but he nodded.

"Mr. Scott. How long have you worked here and what's your position?"

"About two years. I do everything around here—"

Tumlinson coughed. Kate glared at him before addressing Scott. "Give me some examples of tasks you routinely do."

"I clean the cages and fish tanks, I take the dogs out for walks, I bathe them, I feed all the animals. I show them to clients—"

"So, animal care and maintenance of their living environments. Correct?"

Mr. Scott nodded.

"Mr. Tumlinson. Is it correct to say that Mr. Scott has been working here for two years, taking care of animals and maintenance?"

His nostrils flared as he inhaled deeply before answering. "It *was* correct. I fired him last week, but he keeps coming back."

"Can you give me the exact date you fired him?"

"Last Monday, whatever date that was."

"Why did you fire him?"

The man's hands flew in the air as he rolled his eyes. "So many reasons!"

"Give me one," Kate prompted.

"We kept losing inventory."

"Like what?"

"Animals."

Kate frowned at the owner. "Animals went missing?"

"No. Yes." The man tilted his head then continued. "A few went missing: a snake, a rabbit, a couple of tarantulas, and a guinea pig."

Kate looked around the store, unsure how significant those numbers were. From where she stood, she could see at least thirty tanks meant for reptiles and other non-aquatic animals. There was an entire wall with dozens of aquariums. She couldn't see where they kept the "normal" pets like cats and dogs.

"Could the animals have escaped somehow?"

"Well, when I opened the store the following morning, the tops of their tanks weren't properly on. So yes, they could have escaped. But it was his responsibility to ensure their habitats remained closed and secure after he fed—"

"But I—" Scott said.

"Quiet, please. You'll get your turn," Kate told Scott before returning her attention to the owner.

"I understand. Anything else?"

"A few animals died," the owner said.

This nugget piqued Kate's interest, so she stayed silent, hoping the owner would continue.

"But those things happen sometimes. You know, I try to avoid puppy mills, and I do my best to find reliable breeders, but some of them are just in it for the money. The animals they produce are sick from the very beginning. And some of that is probably my fault. I bought a few dogs and birds from a new breeder even though my gut was telling me *not* to. I didn't even go and visit the site. He brought the animals here. I was in a pinch, and I had customers ready to buy a few of them."

With animal deaths spreading like wildfire around town, Kate had to ask, "But are you sure that's why they died?"

"Yes. Pretty damn sure. I took a couple to a veterinarian friend. A dog and a parrot."

"And what did the vet say?"

"With the business not doing so great lately, I didn't ask for the full-blown tests, but I asked for his professional opinion. Once he heard where I'd gotten the animals from, he wasn't surprised."

"And what's that breeder's name?" Kate asked, although it didn't have anything to do with this particular call. Maybe she could relay that information to someone else who could go and investigate further.

"Hold on. I think I still have their business card."

As Kate waited for the owner to find it, she returned her attention to the ex-employee.

"So, Mr. Scott. Do you acknowledge that Mr. Tumlinson fired you last Monday?"

"Yes, but—"

"Now, why do you keep coming back to the store if you no longer work here?"

"He still hasn't found anyone to care for the animals. Did you see the sign outside? I know nobody's taken over my position. Nobody can take care of the animals like I do."

"But Mr. Tumlinson fired you. You have no right to take care of his animals now. You're no longer getting paid."

"I know!" he yelled. "I'm not doing it for the money. I don't want to get paid. I need these animals! They help me."

Now, this is heading somewhere unexpected.

The owner handed Kate the business card, taking her out of her flow for a second.

"Thanks. So, let me get this straight," Kate glanced between the owner and the ex-employee. "You both agree that Mr. Scott here got fired last Monday." The men nodded. "And although you've been fired," Kate said, now addressing Scott, "you've kept coming in to work, but without any expectation to get paid?"

Mr. Scott nodded. "Correct."

Kate turned to Tumlinson. "Is this an accurate description of the facts?"

"Yes. Every day I tell him to go home. To find another job, but he won't. I... I don't know what to do anymore. I won't pay him. I just want him to leave me and my store alone."

"Okay," Kate said, exhaling as she closed her notepad. "Mr. Tumlinson, if you file a criminal trespass notice against Mr. Scott here, then he legally won't be able to come near your business anymore. And if he does, you can call us, and we'll arrest him." Kate turned to the ex-employee. "Mr. Scott, I'll have to ask you to come with me. Do you have any belongings here?"

The ex-employee shook his head.

"Okay. Any store keys?"

Scott twitched, as though surprised by her question, but Tumlinson was the one to reply. "He gave them back to me last week."

"Okay. Thank you, Mr. Tumlinson."

Kate returned her attention to Scott. Since he looked familiar, even though his name didn't ring a bell, she picked up her shoulder radio. Perhaps she'd seen his mug weeks ago during a morning brief. She'd never forgive herself if she let a wanted felon go free.

"Harry-145, requesting a check on Scott, Frank. D.O.B. 1984-04-25."

She kept an eye on Scott while waiting for the dispatcher to report back. His traits were relaxed, no fear in his eyes. *Probably nothing to hide.*

"Operations to Harry-145. I have a Scott, Frank," the dispatcher started. "Driver's license shows address at 194 Hamilton Street. Six-feet one, blue eyes."

"Correct," Kate said. "Any warrant or police involvement?"

"That's a negative, Harry-145."

"Harry-145 acknowledged," Kate said in her shoulder radio before tucking her notepad back in her breast pocket. "Looks like we're all done here then. You have a great day, Mr. Tumlinson."

Turning her attention to Mr. Scott, she continued, "Please come around the counter, and I'll escort you out."

He obeyed, and they both walked away from Tumlinson. As Kate pushed open the door, she noticed the shoelace of his work boot dangling as he stepped out.

"You may want to take care of that," she said, nodding toward his black boot. "And, if I may, I recommend you volunteer at an animal shelter if you need to spend time with animals and are willing to do it for free."

"Ah... What a great idea," Scott said, a wide grin decorating his face.

AFTER FILING the reports for today's incidents, Kate headed home, but not before stopping by a mall on her way. Two weeks to go before her wedding anniversary, so she had to get Matt something.

About five minutes after stepping into the large department store, she found a gift she knew Matt would love, but she hesitated before pulling her emergency credit card out of her wallet.

"How will you be paying for those beautiful cufflinks?" asked the brunette with doe eyes who stood behind the counter.

"Visa," Kate replied, handing her the card and trying to ignore the interests she knew would pile up since she wouldn't be able to pay it off for a few months. "The sign says you offer free gift-wrapping services?"

The woman nodded. "Would you like it gift wrapped?"

"Yes, please," Kate said, swallowing hard. It was as though a giant's hand was squishing her chest, turning her heart to goo. *Stupid societal rules.*

The cashier handed back the credit card, which Kate returned to her wallet.

Why am I struggling with the idea of buying an anniversary present for my husband this year?

Half of her just wanted to do free things for him: serve him breakfast in bed, make a montage of pictures from happier times, or cook him something special to celebrate. But the other half knew Matt's stubborn stand on birthdays and holidays.

To Kate, being ignored and having birthdays go unnoticed year after year while in foster care seemed like valid reasons to want more attention instead of money, but it seemed Matt had grown up to believe the opposite was true. To him, the price tag was more important than the thought.

Who was she to judge her husband for the coping mechanisms he'd developed after his tough childhood? If many lonely Christmases and birthdays had made him crave expensive presents instead of the care and attention that she herself had come to value more than anything, then so it be.

What kind of wife—and future mother of his child—would she be for not spoiling him on their wedding anniversary?

But Kate suddenly pinpointed the real source of her mental struggle.

That Sam woman. Why can't I shake the idea that she's more than a business prospect?

"Here you go, ma'am," the cashier said, handing Kate a beautiful ash-colored bag filled with yellow crêpe paper.

When Kate stepped out of the store a few seconds later, her mind was made up.

She had to prove her gut wrong. No way she'd give a cheating husband a fancy anniversary gift she couldn't afford.

Heck, returning it would just be the tip of the iceberg. All hell would break lose if Sam turned out to be his mistress.

Kate's life would be turned upside down. Her decision to keep the baby or not...

She had to find out the truth about Sam, and fast.

CHAPTER SEVEN

AFTER ISSUING a warning to a speeder on Adams Street, Kate returned to her vehicle. She checked the clock on her dashboard: 3:40 p.m.

Without any urgent call to respond to, she decided to stop by her house to see if she could find incriminating evidence about Matt's potential affair while he was still at work. She hadn't had a chance to do it the previous evening because Kenny had needed her to run errands with him. And by the time she made it back home—after a few card games to cheer Kenny up—she was plain exhausted, and Matt was dead asleep.

But now was a different story. She was in work mode, her senses sharp, and her desire to uncover the truth unstoppable.

Maybe he'd stashed some photos of large-breasted Sam somewhere. Maybe he'd kept a pair of her undies...

Better not. I don't know how I'd react if I found those in our home.

If Matt had been having an affair, knowing about it for certain could ease her mind. Maybe. It would most definitely destroy their marriage. It would further complicate the situation with the baby she was carrying. But what would become of her self-esteem?

That was a separate issue.

The psychiatrist she'd seen for years had done a pretty good job at convincing her that she wasn't to blame for people disappearing from her life, but having a husband cheating on her was much, much harder to dissociate from her personal history.

She parked her patrol car a block from her apartment. While she technically could have parked in one of the tow-away zones closer without any trouble, she didn't want to push it. She was already abusing her privileges by stopping by her house in the middle of a shift.

After walking up the stairs to her floor, Kate unlocked the door and let herself in.

She tried to look at her apartment with new eyes.

The place still reeked of stale cigarette smoke. Although they themselves didn't smoke, they'd never gotten rid of the previous tenant's odor. Even after a few bottles of Febreze, the smell lingered as though there were a secret source she couldn't root out.

She went through the pockets of Matt's jacket, which hung by the door, and found nothing but a pair of gloves, a used tissue, and a spare set of keys.

In the living room, her books were neatly arranged on the end of a shelf, occupying very little space compared to Matt's video game and DVD collection.

That's another place where we could trim the fat. Maybe try to sell some on eBay or something.

Matt's precious couch looked too big for the room and the small side table where the remote and her husband's game controller rested. On the opposite wall hung Matt's flat screen TV next to their wedding picture. How clueless she'd been on that day. Kate could hardly believe how happy she seemed. If she'd known then what she did now about how their relationship would go, she wouldn't have smiled so much.

Physically, Matt hadn't changed a bit since that day. He was still handsome. Kate always thought he looked a little like a young Patrick Dempsey.

But enough reminiscing. Matt could arrive home at any time, so she only had a few more minutes to find something.

Kate headed to the bathroom and went through the two drawers and vanity cupboards. Nothing of note. There was an old box of condoms, and after checking the box and realizing they were more than a year past their expiration date, she tossed them in the garbage. She and Matt had stopped using them shortly after she'd gotten on the pill. That was quite a while back. At least he hadn't used them with someone else...

Kate entered their bedroom. Matt got half of the closet and the top half of the drawers in their tall dresser. She opened the top drawer, where he kept his underwear and socks. Since Kate was too short to see the drawer's contents from above (she normally tossed whatever underwear she'd washed and dried in the drawer without looking), she decided to pull out the entire drawer and set it down on the bed. Almost immediately she noticed the fake back.

What? With her husband's limited woodworking skills?

Surprising.

But there weren't any incriminating pictures or ladies' panties in there. The hidden compartment was empty except for a few sheets of paper and two plastic bags that were rolled up and wrapped with rubber bands. Although the plastic was see-through, there were so many layers of it rolled together that Kate couldn't make out the contents.

What is it? Weed?

She removed the elastic from the first mystery package and unrolled it to find a few smaller plastic bags, which she dumped on the faded comforter. Each of them contained tiny pastel-colored pills…

A split second later, she opened the second bag: a disassembled pill dispenser and glue.

"Fucking dick!" Kate said aloud.

She didn't have the money to have them analyzed, but she didn't need to. It was obvious what was going on here.

What kind of a husband does that?

Aren't these things supposed to be tamper-proof?

She had a look at the pieces of paper he'd hidden. Nothing other than tampering instructions written by an amoral eBay seller.

"Argh!" she yelled as she crumbled to her knees next to the bed.

Her radio screeched for her attention, requesting support from all available units for a robbery in progress.

Although her blood boiled, she unclenched her fists. With her fingers shaking, she carefully repackaged his lies and returned the drawer and its dark secrets to their rightful spot.

BACK IN HER CAR, with the lights flashing, Kate sped to the address provided by the dispatcher while the siren overhead drowned out her angry cries.

She arrived at the scene just as the sergeant ordered support units to stand down. The situation was under control and the suspect had been apprehended, so help was no longer needed. Kate figured she'd have a look since she was already there. She parked diagonally next to another patrol car and stepped out of her vehicle just as a handcuffed man escorted by three of her colleagues walked out of a jewelry shop. The dark-haired man in cuffs towered over the officers next to him.

For a second, she thought it was her husband. The man was about six-feet tall, dark, and handsome, just like Matt, but he was wearing scrubs. She squinted for a better look at his face, but it was pointless. He was too far.

What went down here? Did the man try to steal an engagement ring for his fiancée? Is this what real love makes poor people like me do?

The law-abiding side of Kate took over and shut down her romantic daydreaming. She approached the officer in charge of the scene to see if there was anything she could help with but was turned down.

Kate went back to her vehicle as her thoughts returned to Matt's unscrupulous behavior.

How could he even do that?

But now was not the time to let her anger loose. She had to focus on work and forget about what she'd just discovered.

The dashboard clock indicated that the race she'd been assigned to help with was nearing its start.

As hateful thoughts bounced in her head, she realized there was no word to describe how low Matt had stooped. With his manipulative actions, he'd destroyed every single ounce of trust she had in him.

With her heart stinging in her chest, Kate restarted her car, turned off her patrol lights, and rejoined the traffic, slowly driving past the crowd of casual onlookers that had accumulated nearby. When she finally cleared the group, she sped up and headed toward the meet-up point to be briefed.

At least the race would give her time to digest her discovery about Matt's devious plan.

~

AFTER ATTENDING THE PRE-RACE MEETING, Kate proceeded to the intersection she'd been assigned to block and monitor for the duration of the charitable event.

During the first thirty minutes, as the sun set over Boston, she cheered while watching people of various fitness levels run by her with their four-legged companions. Some runners had taken their kids along. Some had flashlights strapped to their heads; some relied on just the streetlights. At least this part of town had all of them in working conditions.

Shit.

She made another mental note to report those burnt out near her apartment. But screams emanating from the nearby park interrupted her thoughts.

A man spoke over the walkie-talkie, "A dog just fell between checkpoints five and six. He's not bleeding, just shaking and convulsing. Requesting a vet."

Odd. That was probably what those screams were about.

Checkpoint five was just a few hundred feet away.

The walkie-talkie screeched again, this time with a female voice saying, "A dog just fell near checkpoint twenty. Do we have another vet available?"

Dogs don't normally keel over like that, right?

How can two unlikely incidents occur so close to each other?

Then something clicked: the animal killer.

And just as the idea occurred to her, she spotted a little toy poodle coming her way in front of its owner. The dog's strides were erratic, then it tripped, collapsed, and began convulsing.

She was about to report it to the race coordinators, but then got on her police radio instead. "This is Harry-145, acting as safety officer for the Happy Doggy Race in Ronan Park. At least three dogs have collapsed in the span of a minute. The area is packed with runners and their dogs. I'm not sure what is happening. I'll report again when I find out more."

Kate broadcast the nearby collapsed dog on the walkie-talkie, then left her intersection. She would be a lot more useful at the scene.

Another voice chimed in on the walkie-talkie as she made her way toward the toy poodle. "We have another collapsed dog between checkpoints twenty-two and twenty-three."

When Kate reached the toy poodle, she placed her hand on the owner's shoulder. The petite woman in pink Spandex gear was bawling.

"Duke Westshire, wake up! Wake up, sweetie!" She wiped tears from her cheeks with one hand as she petted her furry friend with the other.

"What happened here?" Kate asked. "I saw your dog collapse."

"I don't know!" she cried. "Duke Westshire! Wake up!"

"I already requested a vet. Let's try to calm down. Deep breaths. Did you feed him something special today?"

As the woman in pink grew hysterical, rocking her dog in her arms, another woman spoke up. She, too, had taken her small dog in her hands, and a vertical line separated her eyebrows. "All sorts of people have been petting and offering treats to various dogs. With all due respect, Officer, I don't think Elsa will be able to answer your questions."

Kate nodded and thanked the woman before standing up.

"Shit," Kate muttered under her breath as bloody drool

dripped from the poor poodle's mouth. His eyes were moving erratically, as though possessed by an evil spirit.

Johnston spoke next on the walkie-talkie, first identifying himself, then reporting, "We have a serious situation on our hands. I just saw a veterinarian pronounce two dogs dead. I believe someone's targeting the animals here tonight. Possibly with poisoned treats. Whatever it is, it's fast-acting."

Thirty long seconds elapsed before anyone else came on the air.

Nearby runners, who'd stopped to observe the scene and overheard the last radio transmission, stared in stunned silence, holding their dogs for dear life. Bystanders around Kate started weeping. Hysterical screams pierced the air as Kate tried to reassure them.

But how could she? What could she say that would reassure anyone when she didn't know anything herself?

"The race is officially canceled," a male voice reported on the walkie-talkie. "All safety personnel are to immediately spread the news and instruct people to leave the race and not let anyone feed their dogs anything. Once runners have cleared the path, all race personnel are to report to the starting line as soon as possible."

A series of "affirmatives" filled the airwaves, and Kate lowered her walkie-talkie volume before getting on her police radio.

"This is Harry-145. Following my previous report. The Happy Doggy Race is officially canceled. Several dogs have died. Causes of deaths unknown. No human casualties have been reported, only dogs. I repeat *negative* on human casualties, just dogs."

Then Kate began to follow the orders announced by the

race officials, strongly encouraging people to head home right away.

She returned toward the woman in pink Spandex. She was now rocking her immobile dog in her arms, bawling her eyes out.

It was clear her dog had stopped moving and breathing.

"I'm sorry for your loss," Kate said before kneeling next to her. "I'm going to need you to leave this area now. The race is officially canceled. Please go back home. I'm certain the organizers will be in touch as soon as they have some information to report back to you."

The woman was deaf to Kate's words, but Kate knew it wasn't out of spite. The woman was just in shock.

Kate gave the woman time to register the information and was glad to see the woman's friend coming toward her, her phone against her ear.

The other runners had left, signaling to Kate that the safety personnel manning prior checkpoints had advised everyone of the situation. So, other than helping the woman who'd just lost her dog, Kate's tasks for the race were mostly over.

And just as the woman finally managed to get up, a TV reporter wearing jeans, a white shirt, and a navy blazer showed up with his cameraman. The red light on the camera indicated it was rolling.

Shit. Is this live footage?

"I'm near Ronan Park where the Happy Doggy Race was holding its annual fundraiser to help rescue animals, but this evening turned out to be far from happy. We just heard that several dogs collapsed and died during the race."

The reporter then moved his attention to Kate, his microphone tilting toward her as he stepped closer. The cameraman followed him.

"Officer, can you give us more information?" the reporter asked Kate.

She shook her head, then moved her hand to block her face, her palm facing the camera. "I'm sorry. I have no information to share."

She knew that talking to the media without permission, or without being briefed ahead of time was a big no-no. Handling public relations or any other PR jobs like news interviews was a role left to leadership. Not her. And she was already in plenty of trouble with her colleagues and supervisor without adding this to the list.

No way she was going to make it worse.

Then her police radio crackled again with another report by Johnston, so she returned to the privacy of her vehicle to keep the discussion out of the range of the reporter or his microphone.

She had to talk to her colleagues and see how they were going to handle their report on the race that had gone all wrong.

BY THE TIME Kate parked near the starting line and entered the school where race officials had gathered, the air was buzzing with alarm.

Johnston spotted Kate, waved at her, and then approached.

"How fucking crazy is this shit?" he asked. "So much for a quiet assignment."

His phone beeped before Kate had time to say anything. Not that she knew what to say anyway.

"Argh!" Johnston exclaimed.

"What's wrong?" Kate asked.

"My son. I hate that he has a cellphone. He managed to talk his mom into getting one. He's nine fucking years old! He doesn't *need* a cellphone!"

Kate's eyebrows and shoulders went up, but she kept silent as Johnston texted his son back. Once he finished his message, he looked at Kate again.

"So, he knows about the dead dogs. He's worried about Rory, our dog." He shook his head before adding, "Fuck!"

Kate nudged him on the shoulder with her fist. "Come on. Not much *you* can do about it. A lot of crazy energy around here. You want to step outside for a sec?"

Johnston nodded as he put his phone away.

The two of them exited the building just as a now-familiar face from Animal Control walked in.

"Hey, Jerry!" Kate said, stopping in the doorway, surprised to see him again.

"Officer Murphy... We seem to cross paths a lot these days. About that—"

"No. I wanted to thank you for reporting it."

"I couldn't *not* report it. Hope it didn't make things worse for you, though."

Kate didn't want Johnston to overhear, so she changed topics. "You're here for the dogs I assume."

"Yep. It's getting worse by the day, I swear."

"Didn't you say you hired two other people? Why is it that I only see you?"

He giggled before answering. "I'm the one in charge, so I get to pick and choose who gets what. Safe to say I no longer handle skunks and other stinky roadkill. I choose the calls that excite my curiosity instead. Like the one at your station, and now this..."

"So, what's your take?" Kate asked.

"Crazy. I probably won't be collecting any carcasses tonight unless some of the owners abandoned their dead pets behind, but I had to come as soon as I heard."

Kate leaned closer to Jerry and lowered her voice, careful to avoid being be overheard by the handful of civilians standing near them. "Between us, what do you think happened here?"

"Most likely poisoned. I've seen a shitload of large food bits and crumbs around dead birds, ducks, and squirrels. Probably some really fast-acting poison."

"So, what now?" Johnston asked Jerry.

"No idea. I'll just report to the race organizers. I doubt I'm needed here tonight, but when I saw it on the news, I simply couldn't ignore it. Is the BPD doing anything about it now?"

Kate raised her hands in the air, shaking her head before exchanging looks with Johnston.

"Don't know," he said. "I'm afraid this is well beyond our pay grade."

KATE KNEW she wouldn't make it home anytime soon. Not with the dead dogs. Not with the late shift she'd just finished. But it was for the best, really. She wasn't ready to confront Matt about the sugar pills in his drawer.

So instead, while sitting in her Subaru at the station, she got her phone out and started googling community health clinics and abortions.

She appreciated her uncle's advice to keep the baby, but her husband's lack of scruples and respect toward her changed everything.

With all the debates she'd had to listen and participate in while at school, she never thought she'd find herself in a situation where she'd have to choose. Heck, she wasn't even sure she knew where she stood in terms of whether or not a fetus was a life. But assuming it was, would she be ready to kill another human being to keep her job?

Presenting it as a choice between a job and a human life would be phrasing it very poorly, though.

What kind of a monster would I be for even considering this?

No, job versus life wasn't an accurate summary of her conundrum. More than two options existed, and she'd be able to keep her job, baby or not. Nowadays, the force would get in big trouble if they fired her for getting pregnant.

No, she'd keep her job, but be temporarily stuck behind a desk, pushing paper until she'd physically recover.

The real obstacle wasn't her job.

Her childhood wounds were the real reasons why she couldn't decide right now.

Since Kate had lost her parents so early in life, she couldn't even entertain the idea of going back to work after the baby's birth. Keeping the baby meant becoming a stay-at-home mom, so her baby would get the attention she herself lost when she was only thirteen. She'd have to forget about her dreams, her ambition…

But Matt didn't treat her with respect as it was, so why would he start treating her any differently after a kid entered the picture?

She could already hear him in her head, saying, "Woman, your baby's crying. Make him shut up!"

No, she didn't want that.

Her marriage was falling apart. If she were honest with herself, she'd acknowledge that it had been falling apart for months. Had it been built on a shaky foundation? Did she really know him before they tied the knot? Had he fooled her for two whole years while they were dating?

Where had the real Matt been during that time? Where did the sweet, romantic man she knew and fell in love with disappear to?

She shook her head, unable to answer her own questions.

So many things had gone wrong between the two of them. So many fights and arguments in the last year alone.

The pill tampering was far from the only thing on her mind. There was still that woman. Kate needed to know if Matt was sleeping with Sam. And Kate really had to decide what to do with the life growing inside of her.

Time was ticking.

What if she kept the baby, became a stay-at-home mom, then found out Matt was cheating on her? What if her husband were to leave her and the baby? Would Kate be able or willing to raise a kid alone?

And just like that, the mental image of her dead baby brother popped to mind again.

Would she be able to protect her own child? If someone broke into their apartment while they were sleeping or while a babysitter was taking care of her future son or daughter, could she live with losing her child? She'd barely survived losing her parents and baby brother...

Oh shit. What am I going to do?

And just then, Kate knew.

Instead of going home and dealing with an angry, unscrupulous, and manipulative husband who'd for sure complain about the absence of a hot dinner waiting for him, she would go talk to the only trustworthy person in her life.

∼

CHAPTER EIGHT

KENNY POURED himself some Old Crow whiskey over ice in a coffee mug.

"Glasses are all dirty," he said when Kate tilted her head at him.

Finding this statement unacceptable, Kate got up, ready to help him by doing the dishes when he stopped her in her tracks.

"No, don't worry about it," he said, tapping the cushion where Kate had been sitting a second ago.

She faced him before replying. "You know I can't let your lack of clean dishes go on. And it'll just take a few minutes. Why don't you come with me? We'll talk there."

Kenny appeared hesitant. He looked at the cup, then the kitchen entrance, and then his cup again.

"It'll just take a few minutes."

"Okay, okay," said Kenny before getting up from the worn-out brown velvety sofa, leaving the decade-old butt print visible for the wallflowers to see.

Once in the kitchen, Kate started emptying the sink that

was overflowing with dirty dishes. At least it had yet to reach the point where cockroaches moved in.

I have to come by more often. Not just for company, but to help him clean up.

"So, tell me, what's going on?" Kenny asked as Kate plugged the now empty sink.

She turned on the hot water and squirted in some dish soap. "It's just that I don't know what to do anymore. When I got married, I expected certain things. I had a vision of what married life would be like. Maybe I romanticized the concept."

"Not everything you thought it would be, eh?"

"To say the least." Although she felt tears building behind her eyes, she forced them back by inhaling then exhaling deeply.

"Let me tell you. Marriage is a long-term commitment that comes with its fair share of debates, arguments, fights, and compromises. With the wrong person, it can be a life sentence. But with the right person, it's all worth it in the end."

"How did you know Lucy was the right person for you?"

"From the moment I first saw her. I just knew."

Kate almost dropped the plate she was washing. "What?"

"But it doesn't mean it would be the same for everyone. Not everyone feels this instant attraction, or dare I say love, at first sight." He paused. "Lucy and I were lucky. And times were different back then. Simpler. Much simpler. But we still fought now and then."

Another dish in hand, Kate kept her eyes on the soapy water. "Can I ask for your honest opinion?"

"Of course. You know that."

Kate turned to Kenny. "And can you swear to absolute secrecy? I don't want other people to know what I'm about to tell you."

"Katie, of course. That's a given." He placed a firm hand on her shoulder.

Kate rested her head against the back of his hand for a few seconds. Already, she felt better for coming to see her uncle. She continued dishwashing on autopilot while words poured out. She revealed what Matt had done with the pills and even her suspicions about Sam.

A few minutes later, with the last piece of clean cutlery added to the drying rack next to the sink, Kate asked, "What do you think I should do?"

First, he kept quiet, but then he went in for a full-body hug.

"Katie, my dear. I'm so sorry you have to live with this major-league asshole."

Her uncle's words surprised her, snapping her out of her funk. "What?" She almost wanted to smile. *Major-league asshole?*

"Let's go back to the living room. I'll tell you what I think of Matt. My honest opinion."

With the dishes done and nothing left for her to do in the kitchen, Kate followed her uncle back to the living room.

Once they were both seated, Kenny resumed talking.

"I never told you because I respected your choices. I could see you falling in love with him, and I wouldn't have gotten in the way of love. But this... All of what you just revealed to me... Those actions are not coming from love. So here goes. I never liked the guy. Not at all. Sure, he's charismatic as hell, but he's two-faced. And now we know he's also controlling and manipulative."

"You think I should get an abortion now?"

Kenny shook his head. "No! His being the world's greatest ass doesn't change my mind on that. But maybe you should consider raising your baby on your own or giving him or her up for adoption."

Kate furrowed her brow, considering it.

"It's a whole lot better to be alone than in sleazy company," Kenny said. "While I believe in the sanctity of marriage, I think your situation warrants an exception. I never thought I'd say these words, but maybe you should consider getting a divorce. Especially if your suspicion about this Sam woman turns out to be true. Marriage requires trust and respect. The way I see it, both are missing on his part."

WHEN KATE ARRIVED HOME, intent on having a well-needed heart-to-heart with Matt, she once again found him in the shower and was forced to wait.

This time, she decided to fight a proper battle, which meant getting all the information she could get her hands on.

The thought of going through Matt's private messages no longer seemed wrong. If he'd had the balls to mess with her contraception, then peeking at his private text conversations with Sam seemed fair.

It was the surest way to know if he'd been cheating.

And as she thought about the large-breasted devil, she heard Matt's phone beep, making it easier for Kate to locate it. It was on top of the dresser.

Sam had just texted him.

Miss you already.

Fucker.

Kate entered Matt's password and unlocked his phone, navigating to his text message history with Sam.

The evidence was clear. They'd exchanged naked photos. Matt's engorged dick, then her naked breasts. Scrolling past a long string of sexting messages, she even found a photo of Sam with her legs spread open, her fully-shaven, most intimate parts on display.

Anger overtook the sadness in Kate's confused heart.

How could he?

Why did he?

Is there something wrong with me that forced him to look for someone else?

How dare he cheat on me like that!

With a shaky finger, tears streaming down her face, Kate scrolled all the way to the beginning of their chat, letting the device load up older messages as needed.

She stepped into the kitchen to sit down, as though increasing the physical space between her and her husband could help her manage the situation better. But it didn't. She scrolled through more hurtful messages until, a minute later, she finally reached the top of the conversation. The timestamp on his first message to her was nearly a year ago.

"Fucking Matt!" she yelled. "How could you?"

The shower stopped running. From a distance, Matt spoke up. "Kate? Is that you?"

Kate yelled, "Who else would it be? Does Sam come to our place a lot?"

Something crashed, like a shampoo bottle dropping to the floor.

"What? What did you say?" he yelled.

Ten seconds later, Matt entered the kitchen, a towel wrapped around his hips. His hair was dripping wet, and his eyes shot missiles at Kate.

"What did you just say?" he repeated.

Kate waved his phone up in the air with one hand while she wiped her tears with the other. "You tell me, Matt."

"That's my phone. You've got no right to go through it." His nostrils flared as shades of crimson rose in his cheeks. "It was locked. How did you unlock it?"

"Your weak-ass password? That's what you're worried about? Really? How do you think I set that baby picture before? Fuck you!"

Kate couldn't stand the sight of her own husband, so she tossed his phone onto the tabletop and stared at her feet and the cracked linoleum floor instead.

He grabbed her elbow. "Woman, you have no right."

"Yeah. No. That's where you're wrong. What's going on?" Kate asked while meeting his eyes again.

Matt stared back. "Is this a trick question?"

Kate inhaled deeply before answering. As though anger had blocked her tear ducts, she stopped crying as her hurt morphed into complete hatred for the man who stood in front of her. The father of her unborn baby. The man she'd married.

"I never took you for a stupid person. I thought you were a good guy. A loving, generous partner who would be here for me, no matter what. Isn't it what we said in our vows?" Kate shook her head. "You of all people understand what it's like to be abandoned, to be left without anyone to trust. To lose everyone who matters to you. How could you go and betray my trust in you? How could you disrespect me like that?"

He snarled then frowned at her. "Don't you get why?"

"Enlighten me, wise one. I can't read your freaking mind!"

"Don't you see how you emasculate me every day with your job? I need to compensate for that."

"That's what you call 'fucking around with another woman'? It's *compensation*? My job *entitles you* to that?"

"Hell yeah. You won't let me be the protector. You won't let me express myself and perform my core duty as the man that I am. If I can't be the one you rely on for your security, then I need to be that man for someone else. It's *your* fault."

"Fuck you. I was a cop before you married me. I even insisted on keeping my last name, and you were fine with it. That protector excuse is bullshit. You say it's *my* fault that *you've* been cheating on me? Like I somehow forced you to thrust your dick in between another woman's legs? For nearly a year!" Kate shook her head. "And Sam is probably not the only one. Am I right?"

His eyebrows scrunched up. "None of your business, woman."

"*What?!* Your extramarital activities *are* most definitely my business. You need to put an end to this if you care the least about me... or if you want me to keep this baby—"

"You're keeping my baby. I've waited a long time for this to happen. You finally did your job as my wife. You can't take it away now."

"You're kidding, right? All you wanted was for me to make you babies? You're ridiculous. When we met, didn't I make it clear to you that I wasn't a stay-at-home kind of gal?"

"A woman's place is at home. You're no exception. It didn't matter what you said. It was just a matter of time before you finally saw the light. And I knew I could push destiny in the right direction if I had to."

"By messing with my birth-control pills? That's what you mean? What else did you do to 'force it to happen'? Anything else I should know?"

He winced, probably surprised that Kate had figured that one out. "I don't owe you anything."

Every detail Kate had ever known about her husband had

been proven wrong, or at the very least become questionable. Their entire love story had just crumbled to dust.

If that's how he felt, why had he pursued her in the first place? Had he ever felt any genuine love toward her at any point?

He couldn't have faked all of it, right?

Was it all a big pile of lies? Had everything just been a pile of manipulative lies?

It was too broad of a question to be addressed right this minute. Kate rolled her eyes, clenching her jaw. "I so want to hit you right now…"

He laughed and stepped closer to Kate. Then he lowered his voice. "Do that, and see where that leads you, woman. I've been good to you. I haven't laid a hand on you… yet." With the back of two fingers, he stroked her cheek. "But that can change. You decide."

"Fuck you," she said, before punching him in the jaw with her dominant hand.

His head bounced from the sucker punch, then he rubbed his jaw. The sound of his sudden inhale and the sight of his flaring nostrils sent a chill down her spine.

A second later, he slapped her.

The sharp sting of his palm burned Kate's cheek, but it was nothing compared to the pain in her heart.

These are his true colors.

She'd married *that* guy.

"Shit, woman. Count yourself lucky to be pregnant. You're so disrespectful," he hissed. "I wish I could give you the beating you deserve."

"Yeah? Is that so?" Kate inhaled slowly, trying to calm her boiling temper. She so wanted to punch him again, but she knew it was a slippery slope. She'd never tested the limits of angry Matt, and she didn't want to find them right now. She needed to step away from the situation. Get the upper hand once again. But how?

She stomped out of the kitchen and into the bedroom where she changed out of her jeans and work shirt and into her running gear, including her phone and earbuds.

Matt intercepted her just before she left the apartment. His shoulder rested on the wall by the front door; his extended arm blocked the door, preventing her from swinging open the only exit.

"You're not going for a run now. It's late, and it's dark," he stated in an authoritative voice.

Reaching around his arm and ignoring his remarks, she unlocked the deadbolt.

"Didn't you hear me?" Matt yelled.

She looked at him. His jaw was clenched, his eyes icy. The handsome man she'd married had turned into *that*.

"I heard you loud and clear," Kate said, her eyes shooting darts at him.

She followed the instincts that her police and self-defense training had instilled in her. She twisted his hand at an uncomfortable angle, which forced him to bend his arm and let go of the wall. After elbowing him in the stomach, she kneed him in the groin.

He bent forward, gasping for air and that's when Kate swung open the door and ran out.

She sprinted down the hallway and pushed open the staircase door. Kate descended the stairs faster than she ever had then rushed outside, sucking the air into her lungs. The night was dark and chilly, not unlike her marriage.

With long strides, she ran eastward on the sidewalk, every step helping her clear her mind and lessen her anger.

When she reached the end of the second block, she heard a voice call her name. Kate turned around.

Was that Matt? She couldn't see him, but who else would it be?

What difference would it make to stop and return to him?

No, better keep running away from him. Let him cool off in his own way while she did it her way.

Maybe the discussion could continue between two real adults by the time she got back.

No. Impossible.

Who was she kidding? Matt wasn't going to suddenly change his behavior. Not after what had just happened. She simply couldn't go back home right now. Maybe she could spend the night at Kenny's.

But first she had to work her anger off.

She increased her pace and continued running straight ahead. Block after block she ran, only changing directions when red traffic lights would have let her heartbeat slow down. The rhythm of her pulse gave her the strength to deal with the situation. Letting it slow down would take her out of the quasi-meditative state that running created.

Next thing she knew, Kate passed the entrance of a city park. Without thinking, she headed down the unlit pathway, away from the street. The beats of her current song came to an end, and in the silent lull before the next song started, Kate heard her husband's voice again, far in the distance.

What? Is he still running after me?

Kate stopped and turned around, looking for him, but couldn't see him in the darkness around her. She pulled her earbuds out, to see if she could hear him call out her name again.

Silence.

Until a voice spoke up two feet to her right. "Your phone and your money. Now!" a skinny Caucasian man ordered, his shaking hand pointing a knife at Kate.

She raised her hands in the air, still holding her phone and trying to assess the situation. He was much taller than her. She didn't know if he had friends nearby. His skin was pale, his eyes bloodshot and blinking rapidly.

"Now!" he repeated, exposing missing teeth in his grunt. He staggered forward, his knife now within stabbing range.

He's just a junkie. I can take him.

Kate lowered her phone slowly, leaving her other hand in the air. Just as she saw the man grin in anticipation of getting his goods, her free hand karate chopped the knife out of the man's hand, knocking it to the ground.

The man jumped on her in a rush of rage that surprised her. He pushed her onto the ground and landed on top of her hips then started punching her. She blocked the first punch with her elbow, but the second from his other hand landed right on her neck, causing Kate to choke. Air could no longer come in. She coughed, unable to defend herself. She had to get air. She brought her hands to her neck to protect herself while the man kept punching her, now in the chest and stomach.

Pain shot through her body, but nothing could be done now. Darkness had swallowed her.

CHAPTER NINE

REGULAR HIGH-PITCH BEEPS peppered the air around Kate. Her attempt at swallowing her saliva felt like razor blades sliding down her throat. She coughed, which sent shooting pains throughout her body. The moan that had escaped her own lips surprised her, and the increased cadence of the beeps around her worried her.

What's going on?

"Kate?"

She slowly blinked away the brightness of the lights above her, trying to push away her mental fog and figure out where she was.

"Kate?" the man repeated. She tried to turn her head, but couldn't, her movements encumbered by both pain and something hard wrapped around her neck.

Is this Matt?

When she tried to speak, nothing but painful coughing noises came out of her.

"Don't speak. It's me, Matt. Everything will be all right."

Kate brought her hands up to feel the side of her neck and realized she was wearing a brace. She moved her eyes to the right, toward the sound of her husband's voice.

"You've been beaten up pretty bad, baby. But you'll be alright."

Why is he calling me baby?

Who else is in here?

Images of the man punching her in the park came back, and her brief episode of consciousness faded away into nothingness once more.

~

WHEN KATE AWOKE AGAIN who knew how many hours— or days—later, Matt was gone.

As far as she could see from her peripheral vision, she was alone in her room, and a moot attempt at turning her head reminded her that she simply couldn't—and shouldn't—try again. She wiggled her fingers and noticed a plastic remote in her right hand, which she assumed would emit a noise, or possibly trigger an alarm at the nurses' station.

So, she pressed the circular button and waited.

Would the weird, numbing pain that reverberated throughout her entire body become a permanent side-effect to her injuries?

How stupid was I?

I should have just handed the junkie my phone. I know better.

Stupid, stupid, stupid.

"Kate, you're awake. Good," said a skinny brunette wearing scrubs. Her brown eyes seemed too small for her face. "My name is Ursula, and I'm the nurse on duty."

Kate tried to speak, but nothing came out of her but

strange, coarse, muted sounds, which triggered sharp stabs of pain in her throat.

"No. Please do not try to speak. You'll only make it worse for yourself. I just saw the doctor doing his rounds. Would you like him to come and talk to you?" Ursula asked. "Just give me a thumbs-up or blink once if you'd like that."

Kate made a fist with her right hand and raised her thumb. At least her upper limbs still worked.

Ursula left the room, and Kate decided to see if her lower limbs worked as well. She wiggled her toes. Although she was lying horizontally and couldn't see them to know for sure, she felt the sheets rubbing against her toes, so all seemed well there. *At least.*

The doctor walked in about five minutes later.

"Welcome back," he said as he began elevating the back portion of her bed. "Looks like you were in a pretty bad fight."

Kate couldn't reply, not that she would have known what to say in response to the doctor's comments.

"You want to know what's going on, right? Blink once for yes. Twice for no."

Kate blinked once as she watched the doctor step toward the foot of her bed again.

"Here's what we know." He pulled up her chart. "Your husband brought you here unconscious in an ambulance. You were beaten up pretty bad. You have countless contusions on your body, neck, and face. Your nose is broken, you have four stitches on your forehead.

"It's a good thing the paramedics got there when they did. Your trachea had collapsed, preventing you from breathing, so they had to cut a hole under the swollen area, and they inserted a tube, so you could breathe again. You got what we call a temporary tracheostomy."

Kate's hand automatically went up to her throat. *What?* Her fingers felt the bit of tubing sticking out of her neck now that she knew it was there.

The doctor shook his head, his eyes round. "You're one extremely lucky woman. The punch to the throat could have been fatal. It was so fortunate that your husband spotted you and called an ambulance right away. You must have been born under one very lucky star. You were without oxygen for a few minutes. Based on the CT scan, neither your larynx nor hyoid bone were broken. I believe your vocal chords are intact, but the area is too swollen right now for us to know for sure."

Once again, Kate was taken by surprise. When did she do a CT scan? She was probably sleeping or strongly medicated when they did it. Lots of blurred memories occupied her brain.

"Additionally, you have two broken ribs on your right side. You won't be able to speak, eat, or drink normally for a while. But I expect you'll make a full recovery, and your throat should be back to normal in a few weeks. We should be able to remove the stoma and let your body return to its normal breathing and eating patterns in a few days. The scar won't be big. Just a tiny mark on your neck. Your nose will likely heal without the need for reconstructive surgery afterward. That's the *good* news."

Kate let his words sink in, wondering which part of her long list of injuries sounded *good* to him. Then she pointed her index finger and rotated it multiple times, hoping he'd understand that she wanted to hear the rest of it.

When people talk about the good news, the bad news always follows.

"You understand what I just said?"

Kate blinked once then repeated her circular finger motion.

"Now for the bad news. Your husband told us you were pregnant."

Again, Kate blinked once.

"I'm sorry. The injuries to your body... You miscarried."

Hot tears rolled down her cheeks. Her unborn baby was no more.

Kate had no idea how long ago she'd been admitted in the hospital, but whether it was just hours or days, she couldn't believe she had considered getting an abortion back then. Now that the decision was no longer hers to make, now that the universe—or God or fate—had decided otherwise, she felt an immense loss.

"Once again, I'm sorry for your loss. I recommend you get some rest. Your husband told us we didn't need to contact anyone else, but I wanted to check with you now that you're fully awake and the stronger painkillers have worn off. Is there someone else you'd like us to contact?"

Kate blinked. Once. Twice. Three times.

"Okay, okay. Let me grab a board and marker, and you can write down that person's contact information."

What seemed like an eternity later, Ursula the nurse came back with a board in hand.

"Sorry, the doctor had to go and deal with an emergency, but he told me you needed us to contact someone else?"

Kate blinked once, and the nurse offered Kate the board and marker. "If you write it down, I'll call whoever you need me to call. I'll be back in a few minutes."

And with her words still hanging in the air, the nurse placed the marker in Kate's right hand and left the board on her chest. Thankfully the white object was small and light, but she definitely felt those broken ribs on her right side.

She wrote down Kenny's name and number. She knew a police officer would have been dispatched along with the ambulance, but since she didn't remember seeing one—either in the park or since she'd awoken at the hospital—Kate figured she might as well add her supervisor's name to the board. She didn't know his number, though. But it was saved in her phone.

Shit. The guy who beat me up probably stole my phone.

So instead of a phone number, she just wrote down "BPD district C-11" and asked that they notify Sergeant Bailey that she was in the hospital. In the tiny bit of space left on the board, she also added, "Is my phone here?"

KATE AWOKE to whispering between Kenny and Matt.

They weren't cheerful sounds. More like angry whispers. No. Insults directed at each other.

In semi-hushed tones, the two men uttered words that were obviously not meant for Kate's ears.

While she wanted to scream and tell them to quit arguing, she couldn't. So, she settled on the next thing she could do without using her vocal chords: she hurled her marker at them, and it landed right on Matt's shoulder, making him and Kenny turn to face her faster than she had hoped.

"Sorry, Katie," Kenny said, his eyebrows slanted as he shook his head.

How bad do I freaking look? He's never looked at me like this before. Even when I broke my arm or when I got a shiner in high school.

As she made a mental note to ask for a mirror next time the nurse walked in, Kenny approached Kate's bed.

"I'm sorry I didn't get here sooner. I didn't know until the hospital called me." He placed his hand on Kate's forearm and squeezed it a little, while he tenderly brushed the back of his other hand against her forehead. "Does this hurt?"

While Kate didn't feel pain, per se, the tender touch made her realize her face must be swollen.

She blinked twice.

"That means no," Matt said from the other side of the bed. "One blink is yes, two is no."

"Thank you," Kenny replied while scowling at Matt. "Aren't you useful now?"

While Kate partly enjoyed having her uncle take her side, she could do without the negative energy around her. She could feel their emotional daggers shooting across her bed.

Raising one hand in the air, Kate pretended to write on a board she didn't have, with the marker she'd thrown at them a minute earlier.

Kenny headed toward where the marker had rolled to at the other end of the room while Matt remained where he was.

Yeah. Predictable. Sure, let my elderly, arthritic uncle fetch it while you do nothing.

Kate's heart hurt in her chest, and she knew it wasn't from any of her injuries. Every second that went by showed how poor a choice she'd made when she married Matt.

He hadn't even called Kenny to let him know his adoptive daughter had been beaten up and hospitalized.

Fucking ass.

Those were his true colors, all right.

WITH THE NURSE'S HELP, Kate made her way to the bathroom, so she could relieve herself. But when Kate opened the door and spotted her reflection in the mirror, she gasped, which made her cough, which then caused sharp pangs to shoot through her throat again.

"Are you all right?" the nurse asked, returning to her side as Kate's coughing subsided.

Kate lifted her thumb, but her eyes stayed glued to the beat-up woman in the mirror.

Holy shit.

Her blonde hair was matted, a multicolor bump dominated her forehead, and a vertical cut decorated the end of one of her eyebrows. Medical tape and a metal bar covered her nose. One of her eyes was still swollen from one heck of a shiner.

That explains why I can't see quite right on this side…

Then there was the neck brace and the plastic tube they kept calling a stoma, and which the nurse came twice a day to clean.

I look like I've been to hell and back.

THE NEW NURSE ON DUTY, a handsome and effeminate man named Kevin, checked up on Kate again. The little routine of having her blood pressure monitored, her temperature taken, her stoma cleaned, and her IV fluids replaced distracted Kate from the overwhelming negativity that occupied her mind.

But as the nurse left her room, he surprised Kate with an announcement. "There's a police officer here to see you. The doctor okayed the visit, but I wanted to check with you. Are you ready for a visitor now?"

Kate blinked once, wondering who it would be. *The sergeant? Johnston? It definitely couldn't be Bower.*

"I'll let her in now," the nurse said as he opened the door to exit the room.

Her?

A curvy, uniformed brunette entered.

Ah, her! Larson was the only other woman officer in her

district. They never really talked much. In fact, Kate still had no idea why Larson had ended up on desk duty in the first place.

"Officer Murphy, how are you doing?" Larson said, her expression one of surprise—or horror?—as their eyes met.

Since Kate couldn't speak, she turned her palms to face up, hoping Larson would realize the stupidity of her question.

How Kate loathed small talk.

Maybe there was a silver lining to this injury after all. Not being able to speak had its benefits.

Larson stepped closer and stood at the foot of the bed. "I gotta say you don't look so great. Sorry."

Kate wanted to roll her eyes, but she settled on pointing at one of the chairs instead.

"I will take a seat. Thank you."

An uncomfortable minute elapsed before Larson spoke again.

Come on! Shit or get off the pot. Why are you here? It's not like we're best friends or anything.

"Listen," Larson said standing up again and approaching Kate's side. "Can I call you Kate?"

Kate blinked once.

"That means yes, right?"

Kate repeated her motion then smiled as it dawned on her that Larson's interviewing skills weren't the greatest. Larson's line of questioning would have elicited the same reaction from Kate whether she had meant yes or no.

Maybe weak deductive logic and bad decisions were to blame for her getting a desk job.

"Okay. I'm here to file a report about your attack. Since you were unconscious when they admitted you, the report wasn't complete... Busy officers... Yada yada. Good news is that the sarge is giving me your attack case as a stepping-stone for me to get off desk duty and back on the streets again." Larson made jazz hands and put on the world's fakest smile before voicing an elongated, high-pitched "Yaaaaayy!" that only a teenage girl could have duplicated.

What is wrong with this woman? Kate couldn't resist rolling her eyes this time. *Please make her stop!*

"Since you can't talk, I already spoke to your husband and your doctor." She grabbed Kate's arm. "I know about... You know." Her eyes diverted to Kate's stomach for a second. "Your husband told me. And I'll have to report it. I'm sorry, but that's how it goes."

Kate lifted her brow and made the biggest eyes she could. *Why? Failing to report private health conditions of co-workers isn't that big a deal.*

"I'm still on probation. I can't make another mistake. If the sarge catches the slight lie or omission in my report... So... I have to do everything by the book."

Kate motioned for her marker and board, which Larson must have been briefed about because she immediately reached for them and handed them to Kate.

"Can't you report that I didn't know I was pregnant?" Kate wrote.

Larson shook her head, her gaze stern.

With the side of her hand, Kate wiped off the previous words and wrote some more. "Come on. One woman doing another a favor."

"I'm sorry," Larson said shaking her head.

Everything in Larson's expression and posture screamed that she was. Her eyes were sad, her shoulders slumped, her mouth crooked.

"Thing is, the sergeant already had his suspicions about you being pregnant. He could easily call your husband and find out that you knew and lied to the department by not disclosing your pregnancy."

Kate looked down at the sheets that covered her stomach, feeling tears building up. Again.

"So, I hope you understand. There's no other option."

Kate blinked once, which pushed a single tear down her cheek.

AFTER TRADING her marker and board for the pad of paper and pen that Larson had brought with her, Kate completed her statement for the attack in the park. However, she did leave out the fight with her husband that had led to her running without paying attention to her surroundings.

As much as she hated her husband right now, she saw the man who beat her up, and it wasn't Matt. And she also didn't want to share her marital problems with the world.

Kate handed the pad of paper to Larson, who began reading it right away. While Larson reviewed the statement, Kate figured she'd use the bathroom, so she pressed the button on her remote to get the nurse's attention and began the slow process of raising the back of her hospital bed to a near vertical position.

Kevin walked in, and Kate pointed to the bathroom, so no words needed to be exchanged. The nurse lowered the safety bar on one side of the bed and helped Kate up to her feet. Keeping her neck and head immobile made the simplest tasks difficult. Then there was the assortment of IV fluids pumping into her arm. Based on what she heard the nurse say, one was for pain, the other for inflammation, and she couldn't recall what the third hanging bottle was for.

But, once on her feet, she walked to the bathroom with her assortment of IV fluids in tow. Her broken ribs felt more painful with each step she took.

Kate did her business, and when she came out, Matt was there with Larson.

When did he get here?

The nurse helped Kate back onto the bed and then walked out of the room, leaving her with Larson and Matt, who'd obviously befriended each other already.

"Can we get a sketch artist to mock up the attacker?" Matt asked Larson.

"Of course, if Kate recalls what he looks like, I could get a sketch artist in here today."

Both turned to look at Kate who blinked once.

"We'll make do with her current inability to talk. It may take a little longer than usual for him to get it done, but we'll make it happen."

"And then, the police are going to find him, right? I want to sue his ass. We'll make him pay for what he did to my baby... and to Kate, of course."

Kate's blood boiled. She motioned for the marker, and Larson brought it to her, along with the board. Kate's fingers flew as she wrote words she only wished she could voice aloud.

She turned her board toward her husband. "Matt, you really think a drug addict will have money or an insurance policy? Really? That's your big ticket?"

"Kate, let me handle this. Mind your own business!" And as though he instantly realized how hurtful his words sounded in front of a third party, he softened his voice, gently patted Kate's arm and then added, "And rest, of course." The smile he flashed Kate was the cheesiest she'd ever seen on her husband's lips.

Way to save face, you idiot.

Larson cleared her throat. "I'm going to step out for a few minutes. I need to get myself some coffee. I'll call to find out the sketch artist's availability, and I'll be back in a little while."

Matt exhaled loudly as the door closed behind Larson, leaving the two of them alone.

Matt's grip on her arm morphed into a painful vise. "I saved your fucking life, woman! Don't you forget it. And don't you fucking dare get in my way—"

A beep from his phone interrupted his rant.

Fortunately for Kate, he had to release her arm in order to swipe the phone's screen and read his message.

"I gotta go," he said.

AFTER ANOTHER DRUG-INDUCED nap that featured Bobby, her dead baby brother, along with some messed-up visions of her dead fetus, Kate awoke to Julia, the precinct's redheaded psychologist, sitting on a chair next to her hospital bed.

"Larson told me it might be good for the two of us to chat. Like, I can chat, and you can write down your thoughts... if you want. Blink once if that sounds good."

Kate blinked, unsure where the discussion would lead to, but it would be more pleasant than speaking with Matt.

And what else was she going to do while confined to a hospital bed? She'd been here too long already.

Argh... Shit.

How much was she going to have to spend out-of-pocket on

this? Matt must have filled out the appropriate papers when they admitted her. Was their insurance policy going to cover her extended stay? Or would she get in deeper financial trouble now?

"I know you're not the talkative type," Julia said as she put the board and marker within Kate's reach. "You've never taken me up on my invitations to chitchat at the station, but Larson said I should try again today. Sounds like it's not just your body that's trying to heal now. How are things at home?"

Kate closed her eyes. The last thing she wanted was to air her dirty laundry. But then she felt a sinking motion in her mattress. She opened her eyes to see Julia sitting on the left side of her bed. Julia looked at her with hopeful eyes as her hand reached for Kate's left hand and squeezed it in a comforting grasp.

"This will remain totally private. Whatever you share with me will not be disclosed to anyone else."

Kate wrote on the board. "Larson?"

"No, I told her to return to the station. I'll let her know when you're ready to get the sketch artist involved."

Kate scribbled some more. "Police file?"

Julia shook her head. "No, strictly between you and me. Like, I won't put any notes in your file. Is that okay?"

Kate blinked once.

"Thanks for trusting me. So… This'll be a little difficult, but I'm sure we'll manage. On a scale of one to ten, one being terrible and ten being perfect, how are things at home?"

Kate inadvertently grunted, which resulted in a painful cough.

"Don't try and talk, just write a number down."

Kate stared at Julia's green eyes.

Funny how I never noticed that woman's brightly colored eyes before.

Kate tried to think of some positive things happening at home, but other than the support of Kenny (which also caused a lot of financial strain), there wasn't much that she was happy with. She drew the number two on the board.

"Good. And, like, if you think back to about six months or a year ago, what number would you have used?"

Before the cheating? Before the pill-tampering incident? Before losing an unborn child? Before I knew who my husband really was?

Kate drew the number seven.

"Okay. So, like, things have been going downhill for a while then?"

Kate blinked once.

"Is your husband somewhere in the hospital now?"

Kate blinked twice.

"Do you know where he is?"

Kate raised her brow then, figuring she had nothing to lose, she wrote, "Probably with his mistress."

"You think your husband is cheating on you?"

Kate blinked once.

"How does that make you feel?"

Kate raised her hands in the air, hoping her eyes would convey the WTF answer she wanted to give the woman. *Seriously?*

"Are you certain of it?"

Kate blinked once.

How she so dearly wanted to give him the benefit of the doubt, but the facts had been exposed. She wanted to dig a hole into the ground and bury her head in it, so they could return to the way things were a year ago.

"Larson told me you were pregnant. Is that true?"

Kate blinked once. No wonder every officer at the station

hated Larson. The woman had no business divulging that information to Julia.

"I'm sorry." Julia paused for a second, as though choosing her words carefully. "You haven't told the department. That goes against the department's policies. Why didn't you report your pregnancy?"

Kate let the marker slide across the board. "I was unsure whether I was going to keep it." Reading her own words, she felt judged. Silently judged by herself, and possibly by Julia as well. *What kind of a woman says that?*

"How far along were you?"

Kate raised her shoulders, which made her squint from the pain in her ribs and neck.

Kate wrote the words on the board, feeling the weight of her guilt somehow lighten. "He tampered with my birth-control pills."

Julia stared at the board, one of her eyebrows higher than the other. "Who? Your husband?"

Kate blinked once then locked eyes with the woman, hoping she could telepathically share every detail without having to write them down.

"It doesn't sound like you're happy in this marriage," Julia said.

Kate felt tears rush up to her eyes, and blinking twice made them escape down her cheeks.

"There, there, Kate."

Kate felt Julia's other hand tapping on her thigh while she squeezed the other more firmly. "It's okay. Let's be honest here: you wouldn't be the first police officer to have a rocky marriage."

Kate pulled out her left hand from the psychologist's grasp and brought it to her face, wiping the tears and reopening her eyes. With her right hand, she wrote the words she didn't know she wanted to write:

"I want a divorce."

"That's an irreversible option. Are you certain? I could recommend couples counseling if you want."

Kate blinked twice.

AFTER THE SKETCH artist's visit and one more visit by both her husband and her uncle—not occurring simultaneously—Kate's hospital stay turned into a predictable routine, save for when they changed her tube. Something to do with reducing its diameter, the doctor said.

Kate thought back to her uncle's second visit, during which he'd apologized profusely for not coming by enough, but she understood that getting to the hospital was quite a journey for him. It required ninety minutes via public transport, including two transfers. And with his advanced age, walking to and from the bus stop was quite the effort.

So, she'd told Kenny that he didn't have to come and visit her anymore. It was too much of a burden for him to bear. And the doctor had reported that she was doing well and should be out soon anyway.

As for her husband... Kate could only imagine what he was up to now...

If Matt wasn't spending time with her here after work, Kate could easily guess what he was doing instead. Or *who* he was doing.

So, she spent her days watching the news, and the odd movie if she randomly found one she liked as she stumbled her way through the channels. Ursula, the nurse, even brought her a couple of used books Kate could read. Without her phone, though, she felt isolated. She couldn't go online. She couldn't read her email.

On the news, they mentioned a golden retriever that had been shot dead in a park at dusk while on a morning walk with his owner. The unnamed man hadn't been hurt. Kate didn't hear the name of the park, but somewhere in the short footage that made the news, she recognized a familiar woman: Ms. Edwards, the one who'd called 9-1-1 for a dead cat. Unless the woman spent her days strolling through various parks in and around Boston, the incident had probably occurred in Ronan Park. Again.

Hmm. Could Ms. Edwards have anything to do with it? Nah.

Then again, Kate hadn't run a check on her. There was no reason for it before. Maybe she owned a gun. Could she have been revisiting the crime scene?

As the news moved on to sports and the weather, it made Kate realize how much she missed her daily roll calls at work. As boring as some of them could be, at least she'd always felt in the know about what was really going on in Boston.

She missed work so much right now.

She wanted to know what was happening. She wanted to know if that dead dog was related to the other animal killings, but it wasn't as though she could pick up the phone and call. There wasn't much she could do without her voice.

So, she flipped to a different channel. After a few minutes, she heard something that caught her attention:

"This morning, Boston zoo officials reported that one of their tigers has died. The cause of death wasn't announced, and no additional information has been divulged to the press, but an investigation is underway."

Coincidence? Or did the animal killer get ballsier? A tiger?

The news ended without mention of the dead dog, leaving Kate with nothing else interesting to watch for now, so she turned off the TV.

The zoo is nowhere near Ronan Park. And Ms. Edwards doesn't strike me as a possible animal killer. But nosy? Sure.

Kate closed her eyes. In a very strange way, she was grateful for the lonesome side-effect of being hospitalized. Spending time alone had always been one of her favorite activities. Her forced exodus from home and work was overall a good thing. Her body was recovering. Swallowing had become less painful with each passing day, and so had her bruises.

Her broken ribs and broken heart would take much longer to heal, though.

~

THE FOLLOWING DAY, the doctor examined Kate before removing her neck brace and proceeding with the decannulation, a procedure which freed Kate of her tube. The doctor confirmed her vocal chords hadn't sustained any lasting damage, which relieved Kate since being a mute police officer would have made things difficult... if not impossible.

She had received his go-ahead to try and start speaking.

Kate was about to fall asleep when a familiar male voice echoed from the door, "Knock, knock!"

She opened her eyes and saw Johnston standing in her doorway, a blossoming plant in hand.

She smiled and motioned for him to come in.

"Wow. You got beat up pretty bad," he said, frowning. "Since I hadn't seen you in quite a few days, I asked about you in the morning brief, and the sarge told me you were in the hospital. So, I thought I'd stop by after my shift and bring you this."

Kate put her hands together in a praying position and whispered, "Thank you."

"I'll just put it over here," he said after scoping his options and placing the plant next to the phone on her bedside table.

"The nurse told me about the blinking code. Fun! She said to not ask you to speak too much because your vocal chords were still a little inflamed."

Kate smiled and blinked once.

"I know we're not friends or anything, but... I just thought I should stop by. Things have changed since you got hurt."

Kate moved her hand to the controls of her bed and pressed the buttons until she reached a more upright sitting position.

"Can I help?" Johnston asked as the bed moved.

Kate blinked twice while whispering, "No need."

From her new position, she noticed Johnston tracing invisible circles with his right foot.

What is he worried about?

"What's wrong?" she whispered before exploding into a coughing spree.

"Are you okay?" Johnston asked, standing up and coming to her side.

Kate shook her head and motioned for the board and marker on her nightstand. Johnston handed them to her.

"What's wrong?" she wrote.

"Oh, nothing really. My boy's super worried about our dog Rory. He doesn't want to take him out on walks."

Kate wiped her board and wrote some more. "Sorry. Tough. Any progress on finding the animal killer?"

Johnston shook his head. "No, but the sarge and everyone

in the district are taking animal deaths seriously this time. Even Bower!"

Kate rolled her eyes at the mention of his name.

"Yeah. Shithead Bower. Now that you've been away, guess who's on the receiving end of his pranks and bullying?"

Kate furrowed her brow and whispered, "Sorry."

Johnston grunted and shrugged. "Can't change the guy. But something must have gone down between him and the sarge, 'cause he's been real quiet during the morning briefs."

Kate savored that small victory for a second before Johnston spoke up again.

"So, when are you coming back to work?"

Kate wiped her board again before scribbling her answer. "I don't know. The doc said two more days here, then rest at home for a week. Then…"

She flipped the board so Johnston could read her partial answer before wiping it and continuing. "Then I hope they clear me medically at work."

"Wow!" Johnston said.

"I know. It sucks," Kate wrote.

"You miss it, eh?"

"Can you do me a favor?" Kate wrote.

"Of course."

"Run a check on the Edwards woman who reported the dead cat. Maria or Mariana?"

Johnston frowned. "Sure. Why?"

Kate erased her board and wrote more. "I saw her on the news footage for the dead dog. Unlikely but may own a gun."

"Will do."

"I feel useless here. I'd rather be making the city safer. Helping find that animal killer."

"You and I both. The job runs in our blood, I think."

Kate wiped her board again. "What do you know about the tiger? Related?"

"Based on our latest brief, the autopsy indicated poisoning as C.O.D., but they haven't identified the poison yet. They showed us footage of a steak being tossed above the gate that surrounds the tiger's habitat. Then there was a video of the people in the area at the time, but the camera angle didn't show which person did it. Makes it a little hard to narrow down. They showed us the tape so we can keep an eye on them, but, as far as I know, the mayor doesn't want to release the footage to the media and ask for people to step forward with information."

He exhaled loudly, and then stood up.

"Anyway. Messed-up shit," Johnston looked at his watch. "Listen, I've gotta go pick up my kid. But take care and get better, okay?"

Kate raised a finger and Johnston stopped.

"What is it?" he asked.

Kate wrote again. "Can you check to see if Edwards appears on the zoo footage?"

"Sure thing."

Kate smiled at her colleague and watched him walk out of her room.

CHAPTER TEN

WHEN KATE finally got the all clear to be discharged from the hospital, her husband was all smiles.

But she knew it was just a show.

While signing the discharge paperwork, Kate had asked for the date. It was the nurse who'd told her July 14th.

It was Kate and Matt's wedding anniversary. And though Matt had been right next to her, he hadn't said a thing, leaving Kate to assume he'd either forgotten or didn't care.

After all the required forms were signed, Kate was put into a wheelchair as per hospital protocol, even though she could walk just fine. They both stayed silent as Matt rolled her out of the bleach-scented halls, toward the parking lot where he'd left his car.

So much had happened between the two of them. There were so many things to discuss, but Kate wasn't feeling up to it. So, she kept quiet. And thankfully, he did, too, for the entire drive home.

When they arrived at their apartment, Kate broke the silence.

"You know what day today is?" she asked flatly.

"The first day of you staying home and becoming a proper housewife for me."

And this is where he goes. Predictable piece of shit.

"Fuck you, Matt. I'm going to give you one more guess."

He shrugged then shook his head. "I don't have time for your games, woman."

"It's our wedding anniversary."

"Oh!" He frowned at her, obviously surprised by that little tidbit.

Kate shook her head as she stormed into their bedroom, intent on putting an end to this very uncomfortable situation. After all that she'd gone through, there was no need to stretch this out.

She reached under the bed and pulled out her large duffle bag, which she rarely used, except to hide presents. Matt's expensive anniversary gift was going to get returned ASAP. But that wasn't the only item in her bag ten minutes later, as she stepped back into the kitchen. She'd tossed in everything she needed, intent on not coming back for a few days.

"Where do you think you're going?" Matt asked, pulling his eyes away from the TV as she walked by him to reach the door.

Kate grabbed her keys along with a stack of mail addressed to her. "This marriage is no longer working for me. I'm going back to live with Kenny for a few days."

"Kate, baby," Matt said before standing up. "I'm sorry I forgot about our anniversary. I'll get you a gift tomorrow. Okay? But you can't walk out on me because of that. For better or worse, remember?"

"And the part about being faithful to each other? Does that

ring a bell? You can't fucking pick and choose which parts of the marriage vows work for you."

"I'll end it then. You stay home, raise my children, and I'll put an end to my affair."

Her eyes went round as anger boiled in her veins. "Are you kidding me?"

"I'm serious. I'll end it. Today. Just be the wife I want you to be. Let's go back to how we were before. You'll get pregnant again, and we'll be happy."

Kate shook her head, tears filling her eyes as negative emotions competed in her heart.

"Kate, baby. Just stay home. I promise I'll be a better husband for you if you stay."

That was too much for Kate.

How can he even consider this an option after all that's happened?

"I'm going to Kenny's. I need a break. From us. From all of this," Kate said, making a wide circular motion with her hand.

He walked up to her, and Kate's self-defense instincts kicked in. She brought her hands in and elbows out to protect herself.

"No! I'm not gonna hit you, Kate. If anything, having you in the hospital for so long has forced me to reflect on things. I'm sorry for what happened. I made a mistake. Many mistakes."

Kate shook her head again. She wanted to pinch herself, to test if this conversation was really happening, but she stayed quiet and motionless instead.

"Okay. Go to your uncle's for a few days. I'll end it with Sam. I promise. Then, we'll talk again next week, okay?"

And then Matt leaned in and kissed her, but the brush of his lips on hers, while soft and tender, didn't stir any loving feelings in Kate.

~

SHE MADE two stops on her way to her uncle's: one at the jewelry store to return the expensive cufflinks, the other at a big-box store to grab herself a new cellphone.

With her limited budget, she couldn't be picky when it came to brands, so she asked for the cheapest one available, and the salesman provided it. It even cost less than the gift she'd just returned, which was going to make her credit card statement a little less painful to settle this month.

As Kate parked her Subaru near Kenny's house, she realized she hadn't called ahead; she still had to charge and activate her new device in order to do that. However, she knew Kenny would invite her in with open arms. That was what real family did.

And that was exactly what happened. He accepted his impromptu guest—duffle bag and all—with a large smile and a big hug.

At first, he was surprised to see her on his front porch, which Kate realized was in serious need of a fresh coat of paint. She made a mental note to schedule time to stain the wooden boards before the end of summer, and then she followed him into his house after they'd hugged.

Kate's ribs still hurt like hell.

Driving had been particularly painful—she didn't know turning her head to check her blind spot would involve her ribs —but she was home now. She wouldn't leave Kenny's house for a few days. And she'd load up on painkillers. *Fuck.* She needed a drink.

No more worrying about a growing fetus. Kenny's cheap whiskey would do just fine.

"You can stay here as long as you need," Kenny said.

"I really appreciate it. I'll get back on my feet soon and find a place of my own, I swear."

"No rush. It'll be like the good ole days, right?"

Kate smiled at her uncle, feeling a burst of familiar love toward him. She'd owe him big time for this.

Once her current situation improved, she'd find a way to express her gratitude toward him. While the exact form her gift would take was still unknown, her intention was as clear as the sound of the mini-grandfather clock reaching her ear as it chimed the hour.

BEING on medical leave annoyed Kate more than a little. While she loved hanging out with Kenny and helping him with household chores, she missed her busy days at work.

"How about we go window shopping today?" Kate asked Kenny while they sipped their morning coffee.

"Sounds like that would fall within my budget," he said with a smile before lifting the ceramic mug to his lips.

"Anything you need?"

"Not that I can think of."

Then Kate remembered the faded boards out front. "Do you have any stain left for the front porch?"

"I don't," he said, shaking his head. "Used it all up last time."

"Then let's splurge on home maintenance and pick up some stain after breakfast. I know it's unexpected and probably not budgeted for, but it's much less than what replacing your boards will cost you if we put it off until next year."

Kenny exhaled loudly. "You're right on that. Let me get the flyers to see if there are deals anywhere."

After finishing breakfast and doing the dishes, Kenny got into Kate's car, and they headed up to a strip mall up on

Neponset Avenue. According to their flyer, *Bob's and Sons' Painting Supplies* currently had a sale on paints and stains, and they offered a seniors' discount.

An hour later, a gallon of stain in hand, they exited the store and were returning to her car when Kate spotted the *Exotic Pet Frenzy*.

That's when an idea came to her.

The best gift for Kenny could be the company of an animal…

But she had no idea if her uncle even liked pets. They'd never had one. Their lives were complicated. Adding a pet and the responsibilities that came with it would have been too much back then. Kate had never once asked either. She'd been too preoccupied with stopping her nightmares.

"Why don't we stop in here for a second?" Kate suggested.

Kenny raised his shoulders, and they walked in, the doorbell chiming as they entered the store.

"Maybe we can ask to pet a few animals if you spot one you like."

"Trying to procrastinate, are you? Already finding ways to avoid staining the porch… I know you, Katie," he said, winking.

Kate giggled. "Maybe. Let's just relax for a few minutes and have a look, okay?"

Kenny nodded, smiling from ear to ear.

She followed him without a word, just keeping an eye on her uncle's expression as they walked by the various enclosures. He ignored the aquariums, walking right past the rows of colorful fish, then slowed down when the terrarium section began.

"Weird creatures," he said. "All of them. Why would anyone want a pet spider?" he asked.

Kate smiled before replying, "No idea. I'm with you on that."

"What do we have in this one?" he asked before turning to Kate. "My old eyes can't see anything in here."

Kate looked at the terrarium labeled *Blue Krait*. Whatever that animal was supposed to be, it was either really tiny or it was gone. "I don't think it's your eyes. It looks empty to—"

"Oooh!" Kenny said in the same tone he used when particularly gory scenes came up on TV.

"What now?" she asked, catching up to him a couple feet ahead in the aisle.

He was staring at a snake deformed by something large and round in its body.

"Don't mind it. I fed it a dead mouse earlier," said the petite, apron-wearing woman who stood behind Kenny.

"I don't see the appeal in a snake as a pet. Do you have anything more… cuddly?" Kenny asked her.

"Of course. Come with me. I've got the cuddliest little dog ever. Everybody loves her."

Kate followed silently behind Kenny, who seemed to have a spring in his step as he listened to the store attendant talk about a dog named Carina.

So maybe Kenny's a dog person, then.

As they headed toward another area of the store, they passed the owner, Mr. Tumlinson. He did a double-take when his eyes met Kate's.

Her bandaged nose and the dark yellow bruises that still covered her face—even after her best efforts at covering them with foundation—probably contributed to his reaction.

"You were here a few weeks ago, right? In uniform?"

"Yeah. I'm Officer Murphy," she said.

He blinked a couple of times. "I'm sorry for staring, but are you okay?"

Kate smiled as she brought her hand to her face. "I'm good, thanks. Just a little… incident." Hating feeling self-conscious, she turned the tables around. "How have things been here? Any more trouble with mister…"

"Scott," Tumlinson said, shaking his head. "It's all good now. Thank you. I filed a restraining order, and I haven't seen him since."

"Great news! Happy to hear. Everything else's good?"

"Yes. In fact, I hired a new employee. Bianca's wonderful." And as though perfectly timed, Kenny appeared with a tiny white and caramel dog in hand, the new employee in tow.

"Katie, look at this little thing!"

Under his mustache, his wide grin said it all. His eyes sparkled with joy as he held up a tiny dog with long fur and humongous ears. Kate didn't know what breed it was, but she could recognize true happiness on her uncle's face.

"I know we can't afford a pet but look how cute and cuddly this one is."

"Meet Carina," the female employee said. "She's a papillon. Lovely breed. Full of energy, friendly, and, yes, you're right. Super cute!"

"Ah," Kate said, still surprised by the intense joy shining in Kenny's eyes. "Maybe one day we'll get you a dog."

"One day," he said before lifting the dog up to his face and rubbing his nose against the dog's. It licked Kenny's nose with its tiny tongue, which made Kenny laugh. "Okay, cutie. You go back with this young lady here." He handed it over to Bianca.

"Isn't she great?" Tumlinson asked Kate.

"Looks like it," she replied before lowering her voice. "Out of curiosity, how much for the little dog?"

"It's a purebred. With papers and everything, so just over a grand."

Kenny coughed, probably as surprised as Kate at the price tag.

"Well, I'm sure Carina will find a lovely home. She's wonderful," Kenny said, "but it's time for us to head back, right?" he asked Kate.

"Yep. We gotta go and stain that porch," she said, lifting the gallon she held. "Nice chatting with you, Mr. Tumlinson. You have a great day."

But as they headed back to the car, Kate thought of another solution. Kenny obviously liked little dogs. Maybe they could find an unwanted mutt who would make Kenny smile.

No point in enriching breeders when they couldn't afford it.

The animal shelter may have just the dog for him. And it would be a win-win for both Kenny and the dog.

THE NEXT MORNING, Kate made the call she should have made many days earlier: she dialed 3-1-1 to report the handful of streetlights that no longer worked in her neighborhood. She didn't want to consider whether having made that call earlier could have prevented her attack and ensuing injuries, but she did wish to make the area safer for her neighbors moving forward.

Once her long-overdue task was taken care of, she joined Kenny at the kitchen table.

"You enjoyed holding that dog yesterday, right?" she asked.

He finished chewing his bite of peanut butter covered toast before answering. "Of course. Carina was so cute and cuddly."

"How about we drop by the MSPCA's animal shelter when

you're done eating breakfast? We could ask about getting one of their dogs? They wouldn't be as expensive as the pet store ones, right?"

"Katie, I see what you're trying to do. I appreciate it, but dogs cost a lot in food alone. Then there are vaccinations, health problems, responsibilities... I can't afford one. You can't afford one."

Kate exhaled loudly.

There goes my gift idea. But the joy on his face...

"How about volunteering there?" Kate suggested with newly found enthusiasm. "I'm sure they wouldn't be opposed to us petting a few dogs or cats while we're around. Other than making our way to them, no extra costs there, right?"

"Katie," he started then stopped. He got off from his chair to come and hug her. "This has to be one of your best ideas ever."

After breakfast, they got into Kate's Subaru and slowly made their way to the MSPCA through the thinning morning traffic.

An hour later, they walked into the large, modern brick building. But Kate was taken aback when she saw Mr. Scott walk through the reception, taking along with him a couple as he stepped out of the room.

Guess he took me up on my advice! Good for him.

Kate waited her turn to talk to reception and then enquired about their volunteer opportunities and the possibility of hanging out with a dog or two today.

Judy, the receptionist, handed Kate a brochure and instructed her to sit down and someone would come and escort them to the dog shelter shortly.

Kate grabbed a business card from the desk then joined

Kenny in the waiting area. She could sense her uncle's excitement as they waited.

When a man called her name, Kate turned around and recognized Mr. Scott.

"Hi there," she said.

"Hi," Mr. Scott said before tilting his head. "I didn't expect to see you here."

"And neither did I," Kate said. "But I'm glad to see you took me up on my advice."

"Yes. It was a great idea. Endless opportunities to spend time with animals here."

"Indeed."

"So. Mindy says you want to help out with dogs?"

"I'd love that," Kenny chimed in.

"Let's do it then," Scott said before pointing them toward a door on the side of the room.

THE NEXT MORNING, after yet another quiet breakfast with Kenny, Kate decided to drop by the police station to talk to the sergeant and discuss her timeline for returning to work.

"I know I'm not supposed to be here, but I've been thinking about those dead animals."

"You're off duty, Murphy," the sergeant said.

"I know. I know. But give me a chance. Can you just answer a few questions that have been puzzling me? I'm sure it's information the rest of the guys know. But it's not like Bower is going to share anything with me."

"Fine. You got two minutes. Ask away."

"The dead golden retriever. What's up with that? Any leads?"

"We got a partial fingerprint on one of two casings that were found at the base of a tree. Shooter must have been perched up there. Long-range .22."

The bullet she'd picked up at the dead cat scene could have been a twenty-two caliber. "The bullet I kept—and got in trouble for—was it the same?"

"Yep. I hate to admit it, but your stupid report came in handy. An officer found a matching cartridge at the base of one of the trees you sketched out. But we still can't identify the shooter."

"How about Edwards? I asked Johnston to look into her."

"That came from you?" The sergeant frowned then shook his head. "No. She's clean. No gun. No motive."

"What about the dead tiger. Do you think it's the same killer?"

"Murphy, you're off duty. Stop it with the questions."

"Just a couple more. Please, Sergeant."

He exhaled loudly. "From what the detectives shared with us and the profiler they've been talking to. It could be, but they're not certain. They think he could be experimenting with various methods, see which one he likes better. Which gives him a bigger high or something."

"So, it's a man?"

"No way to know for sure, but that's the profiler's best guess."

"You think the other dead animals from weeks ago—pigeons, rats, and squirrels—were poisoned?"

"Possibly. They've been disposed of, so couldn't be tested. But the detectives think they were."

"Okay. Thanks for your time, Sergeant."

"Rest up, Murphy."

∾

WITH YET ANOTHER day off on her hands, Kate's options were either stain the porch or answer some of the questions keeping her awake at night. She'd done a good job of avoiding thinking about her asshole of a husband, but she couldn't push aside her worries about the animal killer still on the loose and killing pets and pests alike.

So, she tracked down a number for Jerry Swanson from Animal Control and called him up.

"Hi, Jerry," she started. "It's Kate Murphy, from the BPD."

"Yes, Officer Murphy. How you doing?"

"Good. Listen, I'm not calling on official police business. I just wanted to ask you a couple of questions if you have a few minutes?"

"Sure. What can I help you with?"

"Those dead animals. The ones that weren't shot. Any idea what they died of?"

"We started sending the carcasses out for testing last week. I can't speak to the ones before then."

"So, what did they find?"

"Various things. Hard to find a common denominator."

"Top of the list?"

"I'm no chemist, but the odd components, according to the 'plain English' version I requested, are an enzyme called hyaluronidase and a sharp increase in white blood cell count. We passed it along to your detectives."

"What about any other commonality with the dead carcasses?"

"We're talking about so many species, hard to find common grounds, but the vet got back to me just this morning and mentioned dilated pupils, respiratory failure, and wounds in the mouths."

"Wounds in the mouths?" Kate repeated.

"Yep."

"Like kids putting small nails in French fries and killing birds that way?"

"Kind of, but much smaller than that. Between you and me, I got a friend at the zoo, and knowing how curious I am about these animal deaths, he slipped me a copy of the tiger's stomach biopsy report. You won't guess what they found in there."

"Please share, I promise I won't say where I heard it from," Kate said, intrigued beyond belief.

"Tiny shards of metal. How the heck did the tiger swallow tiny shards of metal?"

Kate remembered Johnston's story about the steak. Whoever had thrown that steak over the fence and into the enclosure must have spiked that raw steak with razor blades or something. But would that be enough to kill a freaking tiger? These beasts had to chew on sharp things like bones all the time in the wild, right?

"Any idea of whether the tiger's toxicity report matched your other carcasses?" Kate asked.

"I'm still waiting to hear back from my contact, but I'd bet on it."

"Thanks so much, Jerry. I really hope we catch him soon. Are you going to analyze more things? Like whatever breadcrumbs were found next to the carcasses?"

"You know it! In fact, I just finished writing up a memo requiring any food-like substances be bagged so we can send it out for analysis and narrow down the poison and whatever metal bits are used. Doubt they'd be large enough to pull a fingerprint from, but who knows. We're working tightly with your detectives to make it happen."

"Well, thanks again, Jerry. You have a nice day."

"You, too!" he said before hanging up.

And with those new nuggets for her mind to ponder, she decided to change into an old pair of jeans and get started staining Kenny's front porch.

FIVE DAYS HAD ALREADY GONE by since Matt and Kate had officially begun their break from each other. While she was ninety-nine percent convinced she wanted nothing to do with her husband anymore, a tiny part of her wanted to be absolutely certain she was making the right decision before moving forward.

She knew from experience that most people didn't change their core values, but what if?

What if there was a chance Matt could return to his old self and focus on their marriage? What if he wasn't lying and truly put an end to his affair? What if he became open-minded enough to let her continue working as a cop even if they had a child together one day. Not tomorrow. Not next year, but one day in the far, far-distant future. What if he began respecting her?

It's not as though she'd encountered many men she'd bonded with before. Salvaging their awful relationship could be easier than starting over and trying to meet someone new.

She certainly hadn't had much luck in the love department before Matt.

So, what if...

But what if Kate caught him lying between now and

tomorrow? Then she'd know that their relationship was beyond saving.

Still bored out of her mind in Kenny's house, the front porch re-stained, she decided to conduct an off-duty investigation to see what her husband was up to this afternoon and evening.

But how could she spy on him? He would recognize her Subaru from yards away. She needed a vehicle to follow him around town. The bus wouldn't do it, and a cab was an expense she couldn't afford.

A little saddened by that realization, she walked back into the house, hopeful that some other options would come to mind. She saw Kenny sitting at the kitchen table, scissors in hand and flyers scattered all over the surface in front of him.

"Would you be a sweetheart and return the empty tin?" he asked, his head nodding toward a metal container on the counter top near the fridge.

Kate recognized the box that had previously held the delicious Rice Krispies Treats from Kenny's neighbor.

"Doing your best to avoid her still?" Kate joked, grabbing the tin from the counter.

"Any way I can."

"No problem. I'll be right back."

"No, you won't. She'll keep you hostage for hours. Brace yourself."

But Kate knew she could worm her way out of meaningless small talk, so she headed to the neighbor's house using the side entrance since the front porch was out of bounds for a few more hours while her hard work dried.

Maude received Kate with open arms, inviting her in for a cup of cocoa. Secretly hoping the hot drink offer would be accompanied by more of her delicious Rice Krispies Treats, Kate accepted.

The moment she stepped into her house, the smell of freshly baked cookies greeted her nostrils.

"How's your uncle doing?" Maude asked as she led the way to her kitchen, grabbing Kate's empty tin.

"You know. Same old, same old," Kate replied as she took a seat with her uncle's neighbor at her kitchen table.

"I can make you coffee, tea, or you can have some of my hot cocoa, whatever you like. I've got another batch of cookies that should be coming out in"—she turned to the clock on her oven—"two more minutes!"

"Coffee would be wonderful."

"No problem at all, darling. One coffee, coming right up!"

Kate watched her open cupboard doors and pull out a jar of instant coffee, then fill and turn on the electric kettle.

By the time the oven dinged, Maude had finished her coffee prep, and she put on oven mitts and pulled out a large sheet of golden chocolate chip cookies.

"They smell so good," exclaimed Kate.

"And we'll have some in just a bit! Don't you worry, Kate."

As soon as the kettle whistled, Maude poured a cupful and then mixed in a heaping tablespoon of dehydrated coffee crystals.

"Milk, sugar?" Maude asked.

"No, black's fine."

A second later, Maude placed her steamy mug in front of her on a flowery plastic placemat that matched the rest of her seventies-inspired decor.

"And now, let me bring over some of those cookies."

Maude slid a half-dozen onto a plate that she placed in between her guest and herself on the kitchen table.

"They're really hot. Be careful," she said.

"I'll let them cool off for a bit then. Thanks!"

"Hey, Kate. You must have a driver's license, right? Being a cop and all. Guess that's a silly question for me to ask."

"Not silly. But yes, I do have a driver's license."

"Hmm..." Maude reached for a cookie, but her hand stopped an inch from it. She looked at Kate, then back down at the cookie before finally grabbing it and bringing it to her mouth.

Kate sensed the neighbor had something in mind, so she pulled it out of her.

"Why do you ask?"

"Well, I wouldn't want to impose..."

"Go ahead and ask, please."

"It's just that I have an old car, but I've long lost my driver's license. It was my husband's, see? Now, there's this man who's contacted me, and he may be interested in buying it. I've been maintaining it regularly. It's in good shape. I have a mechanic who comes by every few weeks and drives it around, checks up on it, then puts it back in the garage."

"So, you'd like me to drive your car to meet up with the man and see if he's still interested?"

"If you wouldn't mind."

"Of course not. It's not like I have much to do these days. I'd be glad to help. Tell me when and where."

"Sometime this week, if possible."

Maude got up to fetch the exact address from a pad of paper, which triggered an idea in Kate's mind.

"Maude, could I ask for a small favor in return?"

155

CHAPTER ELEVEN

SITTING IN MAUDE'S LARGE, old, avocado-colored Cadillac, her aunt Lucy's brown pixie wig and a pair of binoculars on the passenger seat next to her, Kate headed toward Matt's office. She never thought her uncle's bird-watching hobby would come in handy for her one day.

But there she was, with decent props, ready to spy on her husband.

Maude had given her permission to use her car this afternoon in exchange for showing it to the potential buyer later in the week, so the universe was on her side. Maybe the doctor had been right. Maybe she was a lucky person after all. Just not in many spheres of her life right now.

Stuck at a traffic light five minutes from Matt's office, Kate donned her wig, carefully tucking her blonde ponytail underneath it. Never had she thought having fairly thin hair would be an advantage, but today's dress-up had proven her wrong. Temporarily adjusting the rearview mirror to look at herself while traffic around her remained at a standstill, she made sure none of her hair stuck out around the pixie brown 'do. Everything looked great. She put on her sunglasses.

I don't look too bad as a brunette!

The traffic began moving, so Kate readjusted her mirror and drove on until she found a parking spot with a clear view of Matt's office's front door. She looked at the time: 3:25 p.m.

Kate knew she could be here for anywhere from five to ninety-five minutes. Matt's sales team sometimes had meetings at the end of the day, so his office hours ended either at 3:30 or 5:00. And, with the universe still on her side, Kate smiled as she watched her cheating husband walk out onto the sidewalk and head to the parking lot next to his building. Kate noted how handsome he looked in his jeans and navy sport coat. He walked confidently, but looked left and right, as though checking to see if someone was around.

"Something to hide, Matt?" she asked aloud in the privacy of her borrowed car.

His red Toyota pulled out of the lot but did not turn in the direction of their home.

"Where are you going?"

Kate started the engine, ready to trail him to wherever he was headed.

He continued driving straight for another twenty minutes, and Kate followed five cars behind him. Then, she saw him signal left, but he wasn't veering onto a road. He was turning in a motel parking lot, and not the most expensive place, by the looks of it.

Should I be thankful he hasn't been taking his mistress out to the Ritz-Carlton?

Although her heart stung, she knew she had to see it through. It was the only way she could quiet the doubts in her mind, the only way she'd ascertain she was making the right decision. But she also knew she couldn't follow him into that lot.

Too small. Not enough coverage.

So, she signaled, changed lanes, and passed the entrance. Kate spotted a fast-food restaurant and turned right. She found a parking spot that offered a good angle of her husband's vehicle across the road.

She turned off the ignition and something fluttered in her stomach. Through her binoculars, she saw Matt still sitting behind the wheel, eyes on his cellphone, right hand typing away.

Texting Sam that he's here? Why else would he be in a motel lot?

Kate scanned the rest of the cars parked near Matt. Nobody else seemed to be waiting in their vehicle, so she returned her attention to her husband's car.

He had stepped out and was locking the doors, the lights blinking as he did. He headed toward the motel doors that ran parallel to the road behind the lot. A brown door numbered twenty-two opened, and a busy woman appeared in the doorframe in nothing but hot-pink sheer underwear. Not only did she have at least D-size cups, but she also had legs that went up to her armpits.

Kate immediately recognized her as one of the two blonde women from the salon.

Kate's stomach butterflies turned into sharp knives.

So, he's the one who ripped a page from my notepad. Stupid ass. And lying son of a bitch!

"I'll end it today," Kate muttered under her breath, repeating the false promise Matt had made earlier in the week.

He approached the blonde bimbo, wrapped his arms around her bare waist, and then kissed her. His gesture was no peck on the cheek either.

Kate couldn't recall the last time he'd kissed her like that.

The pain in her stomach pulsed into her entire body. While her heart thumped hard, her eyes, miraculously, remained dry.

He'd lied to her the last time they'd spoken, even if his words and manner had seemed so earnest. *Fucking liar.*

She inhaled deeply, and then stepped out of her vehicle, intent on knocking on their door to catch them red-handed so he could feel the shame of his behavior, possibly get a glimpse of the hurtful sting that resonated throughout Kate's entire body and heart.

But as she waited for the traffic light to turn red, so she could cross, doubts entered her mind again.

Fuck it!

She crossed the road accompanied by a few honks from cars she'd surprised. She approached the door, her fists tight, ready to expose him. She brought her right arm up, ready to bang on the door, but then realized she couldn't.

Matt would probably deny anything happening unless she caught them in the act—not before and not after but *during.*

She lowered her arm. Through the door, she could hear them giggling. She could hear the bimbo's excited yelps and furniture being knocked out of place.

The walls were paper thin. She'd get a better chance at finding out the truth if she patiently waited for them to be done. So, she headed to the reception area instead, making a note of the neighboring room.

"Could I rent room twenty-three?" she asked as a bell rang above the front door.

The bald, large-bellied man looked up from the newspaper he was holding. "Why that one?"

"Lucky number," she replied with a flirtatious smile. "Is it available?"

The man turned around to look at the rows of keys hanging on the wall behind him. "Yup. How many hours?"

Kate didn't have a clue. "How much per hour?"

The man pointed to a small cardboard sign at the end of the counter. Kate dug her wallet out and forked out enough money to cover two hours then said she'd be back if she needed to stay longer.

The man handed her the key along with a registration card that she filled out under a fake name and address.

With the large keychain in hand and any remains of her pride lost weeks ago, she walked to her shady motel room.

She unlocked and cracked open the door and was pleasantly surprised. Sure, it was a shit-hole, but the place was better than she expected for the hourly rate. Old, worn-out brown carpet with unknown stains and cigarette burns every foot or so covered the floor, which matched the beige and brown bed comforter. She didn't want to go anywhere near it. Kate was certain a black light would reveal too many unsightly fluid discharges. But at least it looked as though the bed had clean sheets. The pillowcases even displayed the crease where they used to be folded.

Kate dragged the room's only chair—a wobbly item— against the wall the room shared with its neighboring unit, the room where her husband had disappeared with the large-breasted Sam.

As expected, grunts, squeaky mattress springs, and heavy breathing reached her ears. And this time she released a stream of silent tears. She closed her eyes and tried to breathe. Even though her mind ordered her to stand up and storm into their room right away, her body simply couldn't, as though paralyzed. By what, she couldn't say, but it was one thing to imagine Matt cheating on her; it was another to hear it happen in real time through a crappy motel wall.

When she reopened her eyes a short while later, their grunts still resonating behind her, she stared down at her wedding ring. Having partially overcome whatever had frozen her entire body, Kate slipped her ring off her finger and threw it across the motel room before burying her head in her hands and starting to sob again. The pain of hearing them had somehow drained all of her strengths. Her original intentions to storm in and confront them gone like dust in the wind.

As their lovemaking came to an end—crowned by Sam's high-pitched squeals and deity calls—so did Kate's tears.

Kate wished for a mini-bar. She knew she'd empty it. But the room was too crummy for that.

Then she saw her ring on the other side of the room, and her harsh financial reality told her she needed to keep it. Not for its sentimental value, but to sell it for cold, hard cash.

As she returned to her chair and placed the ring of broken promises in her pants pocket, Kate heard them begin what she assumed was their pillow talk. Their words were heard so clearly through the paper-thin walls that she could totally picture them naked next to each other in a room identical to hers.

"So, tell me, Matt. Did she buy it?" Sam asked.

"What?"

"Does she think we're over?"

"I haven't seen her yet," her husband's voice said through the wall. "We're supposed to meet tomorrow. I'll know then."

"And what about the money?"

"That? Don't worry, dear. It's been taken care of."

What money? What the fuck are you up to, Matt?

"I'm pretty sure she'll come back tomorrow and beg me to let her keep her job. I've got a plan."

"Run it by me."

"It's simple. I'll beg and plead, then I'll compromise, as long as she switches to desk duty. After some back and forth, she'll agree to it. I mean, after the beating she got? I sure as hell can't see her wanting to go back to active duty."

Oh, Matt. How little you know me. If anything, the beating only increased my drive to make the city safer for everyone.

"So," Matt continued, "she'll keep her job, and continue bringing home that paycheck. More money for us!"

"You know, you should have married someone who made a lot more money. And someone who wasn't as strong-minded. It would've made things so much easier for us."

"I'm pretty sure her uncle will croak soon. No more money leaking his way, and she'll inherit his house. I'll flip it."

"You're so baaaad," she started before giggles took over.

And although the sounds traveling through the wall made it clear they'd once again started making out, Kate stayed put, part of her unable to move from the shock of her newfound knowledge while the other part simply needed to know the whole story.

"You're almost perfect for me, you know?" Sam said.

"That's where you're wrong, darling. I *am* perfect for you. High school sweethearts reunited after all these years…"

"But why won't you leave her for me then? If we're perfect, what's keeping you attached to her?"

"Sam, baby. You know how I feel about divorce. And you know I want babies."

"That's no fair. If you left her, we could be happy together. Just you and me. I'd leave my husband in a heartbeat for you."

"Kate's got fertile eggs."

"She may be fertile, but she's gullible, too! You've made time for me almost every day since we reconnected. Did I mention how much I love you?"

"Not as much as I love you."

Kate didn't know if she wanted to puke or simply die. All of her energy went into staying quiet. Her entire body shook. Her fingernails had started drawing blood from her tight fists.

"I saw her the other day, you know?" Sam said.

"What? When? Why didn't you say anything?" Matt's voice rose.

"Don't worry, dear. Relax. She must have been called to do something near the salon. I didn't talk to her. I recognized her from the wedding photo in your living room."

"I don't like the idea of you and her together. Even if you didn't talk to her."

"You certainly picked the small, sporty model! I thought you liked my curves. It made me wonder what you originally saw in her."

"You know how much I love your humongous tits, babe. But Kate's the one I connected with. For some reason, she bonded with my orphan story."

"Yeah. Proving my point exactly. Gullible as hell. How's your dad, by the way?"

WITH HER HAND covering her muted cries, Kate ran from the room. She didn't bother to close the door or return the key, which she'd tossed on the bed.

Zigzagging her way through the traffic—this time not waiting until cars slowed down—she ran back to her neighbor's Cadillac.

She'd been fooled by a low-level conman for years?

Four fucking years!

And what fucking money were they talking about?

She wiped the tears from her eyes and started the engine, eager to find the closest ATM. If only she'd upgraded her data plan on her new phone... She could have checked the balance there...

But five minutes later, she spotted her bank's logo on an illuminated sign on the side of the road, so she veered off and headed toward the entrance.

After waiting in line behind an elderly woman for what seemed like an eternity, Kate finally got her turn at the machine.

She stepped forward the instant the woman had cleared the space. Kate slid her card in, entered her PIN, and then braced herself as she pressed the button to see the balance on their joint account, the one that supposedly held their down payment for a house she now knew they were never going to get.

A second later, the screen displayed a number that made her punch the machine and yelp out in pain:

$18.02

She printed out a receipt, just so she'd have proof, then drove herself to the police station, her eyes shiny and crimson from crying, but she couldn't care less anymore. The bastard needed to get arrested. And she sure as hell didn't want to be the one doing it.

Her two-timing con husband was the one person she didn't want to see ever again.

~

CHAPTER TWELVE

AFTER A FULL FORTY-EIGHT hours that Kate spent in bed feeling sorry for herself and swearing at her gullibility, Kenny convinced her to leave the house and get some fresh air.

"It'll do you good."

Kate knew her uncle was right, but she upgraded her phone plan first, just so she'd have access to the Internet while he'd temporarily booted her out of the house.

She decided to head toward Jamaica Pond and take in the serene atmosphere of nature for a change. If only the department had cleared her for work... Patrol would help take her mind off of Matt.

But ducks would have to do for today.

Even though every couple that walked by caused a pinch in her heart, she pushed through. She walked until she came to a bench that was unoccupied.

She sat. She inhaled deeply, resisting the urge to allow tears to come out once more.

Her eyes lingered on the pond that stretched in front of her.

Off to one side, the path continued, with a few people feeding ducks about a hundred yards away.

Ducks. These ones had obviously been lucky enough to have been spared by the animal killer, whoever he was.

Weren't ducks fortunate creatures? They didn't have to deal with heartbreaks and deception. But who knows... Maybe ducks had relationships, too. Kate had no idea.

She let her gaze rest on one particularly brave duck who was making its way toward a man holding a large piece of food.

From where she sat, Kate couldn't tell if it was bread or something else, but it was definitely large for a breadcrumb. Then she wondered why the man wore gloves. It wasn't cold at all.

Then she noticed the red shoes he wore.

I've seen those shoes before.

But the man's face wasn't visible from where Kate sat. She could, however, see his blond hair. Although he was hunched over, she'd guess he was around six-feet tall. Based on how his clothes hung off of him, with the loose fabric of his sleeves flapping in the wind, the man was scrawny.

When a memory flashed through her mind, she pulled out her phone, found Johnston among her contacts, and sent him a message:

**The video from your son with dead pigeons.
Can you forward it to me?**

A minute later, her phone beeped.

She watched the clip and saw bright red shoes. Although she couldn't tell for sure the shoes were the same from this far away, how many people wore red freaking shoes nowadays?

Then she remembered the dead cat and the chubby woman

who'd called 9-1-1 instead of 3-1-1. Among the group of bystanders that had gathered around the cat... That's where she'd seen him before. That's where she'd seen Scott!

Kate knew fair well that killers and other sociopaths often revisited crime scenes. Scott had stuck around. With the pigeons, and with the cat.

Could it be?

Then Kate shook her head. She had no real evidence. Red shoes and wrong place at the wrong time. Coincidences.

But then she thought of the animal shelter. She looked through her call history, found the number, and waited as the ringtone sounded again and again. Finally, someone answered.

"Hi, this is going to sound strange, but could you tell me if you've noticed an increase in the number of deaths at the MSPCA?"

"Who's this?" the receptionist asked.

"My name's Kate Murphy."

"Are you with the press?"

"No, no. I just want to know, out of curiosity."

"I'm afraid I can't answer this question, but if you leave your name and number, I can have someone call you back."

Kate did just that, all the while thinking that the receptionist's answer was a cover-up until a trained PR person could answer it without incriminating anyone. So, Kate read the response as a "more than likely."

In the distance, the brave duck reached Scott and snapped the food offering into its beak before taking it down to the ground. The morsel was big but obviously tasty based on how intently the duck ate it.

The duck's head bobbed strangely as it finally swallowed the bite then walked back toward the pond and its feathered mates.

A nearby boy who'd seen the exchange between Scott and the duck approached Scott.

Probably wants to feed the ducks, too.

Kate was pretty sure the MSPCA wouldn't call her back right away, but she couldn't resist following up on her suspicions.

It could be.

What if?

Her thumb flew across the screen as she researched what the animal missing from the pet store was. After Google reported that blue kraits were striped snakes from Malaysia, she looked into the effects of their venom. Then she googled tarantula bites.

Fucker.

While she had no idea if the man owned a gun, he certainly had access to the venom. And with his experience handling exotic snakes and spiders, he probably knew how to extract it. He could have stolen those animals. Then it was just a matter of putting the venom into food.

Kate looked up again and saw Scott talking to the boy, offering him a piece of whatever he had in his plastic bag. The two appeared to be chatting, pointing at the ducks on the pond. Kate couldn't hear what they were saying, but her instincts told her Scott was up to no-good.

She texted Johnston again.

I think I found him. The animal killer.

What?

**Come to Jamaica Pond ASAP.
He's here.**

Near the boathouse.

She knew the park was outside their district, but she was off duty. Calling 9-1-1 and trying to explain herself would be a waste of time. Johnston could do a lot more and a lot faster than she could right now.

And as she brought her eyes up from her device, she spotted the boy about to put the food into his mouth.

"No, drop that!" she yelled at the top of her lungs, which made her cough. Her vocal chords hadn't fully healed just yet.

The man turned toward her, and so did the boy. Thankfully, he obeyed, but the man took off running, leaving the bag behind.

She jumped up and began pursuit. "Stop, now!" she yelled as she followed the path and started to bridge the hundred-yard gap between them.

A few seconds later, she bent down to pick up the bag he'd dropped earlier, and then continued. While her broken ribs hurt like hell, she pushed through the pain. She made good progress. Sure, her pace was nowhere near her regular performance, but she was steadily gaining on him.

Fifty yards.

"Scott! Drop to the ground. Now!"

But he didn't. Instead, his body knocked over a woman coming from the opposite direction.

Shit. Hope she's okay, Kate thought before ignoring her and refocusing on Scott, now thirty yards ahead.

When he stumbled, Kate seized the opportunity and tackled him, which made her yelp in pain. It hurt worse than hell this time.

"Shit!" she swore as she used the weight of her body to pin

Scott on the ground, face-first. She dropped the bag she'd been carrying so that she could clutch her ribs.

Fuck that hurts.

She coughed.

Maybe the doc had a point when he said I wasn't ready for duty yet.

"Will you get off me?" Scott said. "I didn't do anything wrong."

"Is that so?" Kate said, realizing that passersby had stopped to stare. A young man had his cellphone out in front of him, more than likely recording what was happening.

I certainly hope I'm right, Kate thought to herself just as a broad-shouldered patrol officer on a bicycle arrived at the scene.

"What's going on here?" he asked authoritatively.

Kate raised both her hands in the air but stayed atop Scott.

"Ma'am, can you please get off of him?"

"I'm Officer Murphy from C-11," she said looking at the officer's nametag, which read Harrison. "I'm off duty, but I believe this is the man we've all been looking for. The one who's been killing animals in and around Boston. I can get off of him, but I don't want him to get away. I'm in no condition to try and catch him if he runs again."

Harrison frowned at her before reaching for his shoulder radio. A minute or so later, after some back and forth with his supervisor, Officer Harrison proceeded to cuff Mr. Scott.

∾

CHAPTER THIRTEEN

"MURPHY, HAVE A SEAT," said Sergeant Bailey.

Kate obeyed, sitting across the desk from her supervisor.

As though a movie played in her mind, she thought about all the times she'd sat right here across from him during the last few weeks.

Way too many times for a single police officer.

But with her morning sickness episodes gone for good, and with Bower's pranks far less likely to happen, she was hopeful her one-on-ones with the sergeant would become less frequent.

"The meaning of being 'on leave' didn't sink in through your thick skull, I take it."

Fuck, here it goes again.

"But, Murphy,"—he shook his head—"your theory checked out. I don't know how you connected dots that the detectives didn't, but you did it. So, good work. They found a long-range rifle with a silencer. The ballistic report came back positive. They found the snake and spiders…"

Kate was anxious to ask about getting her badge and gun

back, but she didn't want to put her foot in her mouth, so she kept quiet.

"All these years," he continued, his head shaking. "Who knew my mother's Halloween warnings about razor blades hidden in apples would be something I encountered at work in Boston. But this guy certainly took it up a notch, lacing food with pins and tiny shards of razor blades and a blend of snake and spider venom. Nothing like a fresh wound in your mouth to ensure the toxins make it straight into your bloodstream instead of being neutralized in your stomach. Well, he's off the streets now, thanks to you, Murphy."

"So, does that mean I'll be reinstated?" she asked, unable to help herself.

"We obviously can't keep you away from the job. I'm reinstating you, but only for desk duty."

"Like Larson? But Sergeant—"

"For now!" His brown eyes were stern as he continued. "It's simply not my call. The doc hasn't cleared you yet is all."

He stood behind his desk, indicating the end of their meeting.

"And for the record," he added as Kate got on her feet, "you're nothing like Larson. You're a good cop. With a hell of a lot of potential."

ON HER WAY home from the station, Kate stopped by a liquor store to grab a bottle to celebrate her reinstatement at work.

Just as she was browsing through the low- to mid-range whiskey, her phone beeped with a message from her newly acquired divorce lawyer.

He's been served.

"Yay!" she said aloud. A short and stubby Hispanic man turned to squint at her, but Kate couldn't care less.

Instead, she turned her gaze to the next shelf up, which held a much better selection to choose from.

The hell with it. This day is worth celebrating! And Kenny's going to love my gift this time.

KENNY WALKED from the kitchen to the living room with two tumblers in hand, each containing a single ice cube. He sat down on the couch next to Kate then put the glasses near the bottle in front of them.

"I can't believe you splurged on a bottle of Jameson Gold Reserve," he told Kate.

"We only live once, and we have multiple reasons to celebrate today," she said. "I don't know if I'll get any money out of this divorce when all is said and done, but one thing's for certain: my own money will no longer be used to pay for fancy meals, hotel rooms, or other things I never even partook in!"

"Hear, hear." Kenny poured a finger of the amber liquid in each glass.

"To this hell finally being over," Kate said, raising her drink.

Kenny met her eyes, raised his glass, but then pulled it back toward him and paused. "No, Katie. To the start of a new chapter in your life. You've got a great future ahead of you. I just know it," he said, clinking his drink against Kate's. "To a bright future."

Kate repeated the words and smiled at her uncle before

bringing the rich, layered liquid to her lips and enjoying the warmth of it sliding down her throat.

"Shall we?" he asked her, excitement in his eyes.

Kate nodded as she got comfortable on the old couch next to him.

Kenny pressed play on his VCR remote, and an old episode of *Adam-12* played on Kenny's old TV set.

As the familiar characters appeared on the screen, she couldn't help but reflect on her own life.

Who knew what would happen now...

With Matt out of the picture, she'd lost a part of herself, but it was an infected part. It had to go. She'd spend less time worrying about her home life. She'd be able to focus on work moving forward.

And that was all good.

As for the life she'd lost...

She briefly rubbed her stomach then decided that she wouldn't dwell on it. It was probably for the best as well. She moved that sad memory into the same mental drawer where the pictures of her murdered family resided.

Since nothing could be done about it, she decided to move on and swore to herself to never let it become another endless source of nightmares for her.

Kate had enough tangible, life-or-death problems. She couldn't afford the luxury of obsessing over the troubles that only lived in her mind.

So, after sipping her whiskey, she leaned her head against Kenny's shoulder, letting his presence reassure her the way it had done so throughout her teenage years.

He stretched his legs out on the ottoman in front of him and then wrapped his arm around Kate before gently tapping her on the shoulder.

"Everything's gonna be just fine. I've got you. You've got me." After a short pause, Kenny added. "And if all fails, we've got Jameson."

Kate smiled.

Everything's gonna be just fine.

~

THE END

PLEASE REVIEW THIS BOOK HERE:
https://www.amazon.com/review/create-review/asin=B07C5BZHPF

EXCERPT FROM THE LAST HOPE

CHAPTER 1

Kate Murphy
Secret Hiking Spot, Maine

WARM, salty air kissed Kate Murphy's freckled skin as she sat, perched in surroundings that embodied her emotions.

Early summer rays bombarded the ocean, forming tiny diamonds that sparkled in the distance. Mere minutes later, the same peaceful, glistening water would morph into powerful waves that crashed onto the jagged rocks one hundred feet below Kate's dangling legs, pulverizing any debris that may have been floating along for the ride. She sipped her bottle of water while soaking in her favorite scenery. The soft chirps and warbles of a few birds accompanied her thoughts.

Life was pretty good these days, even though Kate's latest attempt at becoming a detective had been rejected yet again, but at least now she was part of a different district. It meant fresh opportunities and new people. Maybe her next application would be approved.

Kate stood up, finished her drink, and then returned the empty stainless-steel bottle to her backpack. It clunked against her phone, which she dug out: it was 1:03 p.m. Five missed calls and one voicemail.

Weird.

The message must have come in during the past hour when she came into range. All she ever got around here was one bar, and it only appeared if the winds were blowing in the right direction (with no clouds on the horizon) and lucky leprechauns sprinkled their magical signal-boosting powder around her.

Crappy coverage.

She should change cell providers. Then again, there was something to be said for enjoying quiet time and being unreachable, especially when she was here.

She tapped her way to the voicemail screen. Unknown number. She pressed "play" and listened to it over speakerphone.

"Miss Murphy, I'm calling on behalf of Kenneth Murphy. My name's George Hudson, and I'm the defense attorney who's been assigned to your uncle's case. He's been arrested. He wanted me to let you know he's currently being held at the Roxbury Precinct, accused of murder. Your uncle says he's innocent, and I'll do my best to prove that he is. Sorry for leaving this important message on voicemail. I would have preferred doing it in person, but your uncle said I might have a hard time reaching you, and I didn't want to wait too long. I'll give you a call later this week with more details."

What?

Kate jumped to her feet, staring at her now-silent phone. Had she heard that right?

She listened to the message again, this time with the phone pressed against her ear.

She had to head back if she wanted to get enough cell coverage to do anything. Kate stuck her phone back in her bag, strapped it on tightly, and then ran the three miles she'd just hiked, back to her car.

When she reached her Subaru, it was already 1:45 p.m. She was starting to regret her decision to drive out-of-state on her day off. She was 170 miles away from the Roxbury station.

Kate drove fast on the winding, scenic roads, ignoring the breathtaking views she would usually savor. She far exceeded the speed limit, mastering the unpaved bends like a professional race car driver. The skills she'd honed during police training certainly made driving her Impreza even more fun than before, but this time her mind was on autopilot.

Why was Uncle Kenny accused of murder? He was the last of her living relatives, the only human being she felt connected to and loved by. He couldn't have killed anyone.

After fifteen years of psychotherapy, Kate was mostly over the gory memories of finding her own mother, father, and little brother murdered in their family home, throats slit, her mother half-naked and raped, and blood dripping down the kitchen walls.

Today was June 23rd, the twentieth anniversary of that awful day. It was why she'd requested—and had been granted —a day off.

Kenny, her dad's older brother, had taken Kate in when she was thirteen years old. He didn't have children of his own, so he and his wife, Lucy, had decided to adopt her. They'd done the best they could to protect and help her get over her horrible loss and trauma. The therapist's bills had been expensive, especially on Kenny's welder's salary. Lucy's chain-smoking had quickly ruined her health. She'd died of lung cancer when Kate was twenty-three. Tragedies seemed to occur every decade for

Kate, and now, at the age of thirty-three, her uncle was in jail. And for murder? Kenny was all she had left in the world.

He couldn't have killed another person, could he? No, no way.

A white-tailed deer crossed the road two hundred feet in front of her, snapping Kate's attention away from the past and returning it to the present. She knew this part of the countryside like the back of her hand. Another two miles and she'd be on paved roads, and then it'd be five more miles to the state highway where she could get decent cell reception.

When she finally reached the end of the cellular dead zone, Kate pressed the voice command on her steering wheel.

"Call the district commander at the Roxbury police station."

Siri confirmed her request, and then Kate heard a ringing sound, followed by Susan's British accent. "Captain Cranston's desk. How may I be of service?"

"Hi, Susan. It's Officer Murphy."

"Yes. Kate, right?"

"Yeah. I got a voicemail from a lawyer saying my uncle, Kenny Murphy, has been brought in for murder and he's being held at our station. Can I talk to the district commander and find out what's going on?"

"He's in a meeting right now, and there's a queue of people waiting to see him, but I'll let him know you called."

Kate tapped her fingers on her steering wheel and shook her head.

A message wouldn't do much to help Kenny... but that's all Susan could do.

"I'm on my way to the station. I should be there in about two hours. Do you think he'll still be around?"

"I don't know, love. Unsure how long his meeting will be, but doubtful he'll stick around after it's over and he's done seeing these other fine folks. But who knows? You might be able to catch him on his way out. I'll leave him a note to call you back ASAP."

"Thanks, Susan."

Kate returned her focus to the road, sneaking intermittent glances at the phone in her cup holder, and hoping he'd call her back. Then again, why would he? That wasn't proper. She wasn't following the chain of command. She had no right to go to him directly. As far as she knew, there was no official police handbook designating the appropriate person for police officers to talk to when their loved ones were arrested for murder. When she'd first joined the district, Capt. Cranston had told her that his door was always open. She hoped he'd meant it.

A giant billboard promoting Clark Ferguson, a handsome, brown-haired Boston mayoral candidate with a million-dollar smile, welcomed her to Massachusetts. Kate still had a solid hour of driving to get to Roxbury and traffic could be wicked bad. She checked the clock on her dash again: 3:30 p.m.

Today's Tuesday.

She might just get there in time to see Capt. Cranston before he left for the day.

SEVENTY-FIVE MINUTES LATER, Kate veered into the station's lot, parked her car, and then ran three flights of stairs to the district commander's office, only to find it empty and locked.

Shit. Too late.

She wouldn't be able to hear the official word on Kenny's arrest, but she should still be able to talk to her uncle and learn what they'd told him and see if he was doing okay. The poor man was probably scared to death.

She made her way down to the detention area and found the officer on duty; his name tag read "Reynolds." She recognized his face but couldn't remember his first name.

Dave? Don? Dean? One of those "D" names.

"Hey, Reynolds."

"Hey, Murphy. What brings you here? Aren't you supposed to be taking a few days off?"

She smiled. She'd only been here a couple of weeks, but being a female officer seemed to help her male counterparts remember her name... and her schedule? Maybe it had nothing to do with being a woman in a man's world. Wasn't it always easier for any group to remember the new kid's name?

"Today was my only day off. I got a message telling me my uncle has been arrested and is being detained here. Do you have a Murphy in the cell?"

"Let me see. I'm just here for a few minutes covering for Matthews. Bad burrito," Reynolds said with a laugh. He then looked at Kate and became serious again. He returned his attention to the computer screen. "Don't know who he's got in here. Let's see... Kenneth Murphy?"

"Yeah, that's him. Can I see him?" Kate asked.

"Sure, do you need an escort?"

She shook her head. "He's my uncle, no need."

Reynolds nodded and stood to open the door. "You know the drill. Leave your stuff here."

Kate emptied her pockets and left her backpack with him. Reynolds and Kate then walked over to Kenny's holding cell, their footsteps echoing against the bare, white concrete walls. An antiseptic smell reminded her of her last hospital visit. Most cells were unoccupied, and Kate soon spotted her uncle's balding head a few feet away. He was sitting on a jail bed, staring at the floor in front of him. What was left of his hair was restless and out of place. His white mustache had seen better days.

"Kenny!"

He looked up, eyebrows raised, faint dimples appearing on his cheeks from his growing smile.

"Katie, sweetie. I'm so glad to see you."

"Mr. Murphy, please put your back against the wall," Reynolds said. After her uncle complied, Reynolds unlocked the door to let Kate in, relocked it, and then addressed her on his way out. "Holler when you're done. Fifteen minutes max. Matthews will be back shortly."

Kate hugged her uncle. He was seventy-six years old and frail, but his arms held onto her like she was a lifebuoy in a violent storm.

She sat next to him on the bed and looked into his tired, brown eyes. They seemed sadder than usual and confused.

She tapped his leg and gently squeezed his knee, "How are you holding up?"

He answered by raising his shoulders and shaking his head, his mouth forming an upside down U.

"Tell me everything," Kate asked.

"I don't know what happened. Why do they think I killed that man? That's the craziest shit I've ever heard."

"Tell me about the arrest."

"They showed up at my house this morning. Two plainclothes officers with a warrant and four or five uniformed men."

"What did they say?" Kate asked.

"They wanted to know if I was Kenneth Sam Murphy, so I

told them I was. Then, they said I was under arrest for the murder of Paul McAlester."

"Who?"

Kenny's eyes widened. "That's what I said! But one of them got ahold of my wrists and handcuffed me while they read me my rights. They said they had a warrant to search the house. I was too dumbfounded to remember anything else they said after that. Next thing I know, I'm being questioned about what I did three nights ago."

"What did you say?"

"I said I didn't remember, but I probably heated my dinner and watched a movie while drinking a scotch or two."

"You don't remember?"

Kenny shook his head, and Kate felt a black curtain of despair fall over them.

He has no alibi.

"I'm getting old. Most nights blend into one," he said. Then, he gazed at Kate's face, softening some as he smiled at her. "You don't come and visit often enough. All I have left are memories. Some good, some bad. Lately, the awful ones have been on the reel, and I drink to shut them down. Normally works for a few hours until I fall asleep."

Kate hugged her uncle again, feeling guilty for not being there for him more often. Her failed marriage had been at the forefront of her mind lately, and she had needed more alone time than usual. And then the anniversary of her family's murder... That was no excuse, though. Her uncle didn't deserve to be neglected just because she couldn't get her shit together.

"I'm so sorry. I'll make things right. I'll talk to the district commander tomorrow and see if I can find out something new that could help us."

Kenny nodded, and he scratched the back of his neck. A forced smile appeared under his mustache. Kate knew that look too well. It meant he was terrified, just like when he'd found out about his wife's cancer and how large her medical bills were going to be. Kate knew better than to tell him to voice his feelings. No way would an old, Irishman like him spill the contents of his heart.

Changing subjects was always the best option when he scratched his neck or faked a smile.

"I got a call from your lawyer," Kate said. "How did you find him?"

"You know I can't afford one, so they assigned him to me. Seems nice enough."

Kate knew how tight her uncle's finances had been, and still were. He'd been poor for the past twenty years. He ate lots of canned beans and could barely keep the heat on some months. Once again, guilt got ahold of her. She should have given him more than ten percent of her paychecks. He deserved more; especially after all he'd done for her. But she didn't make that much, and the job forced her to live in Boston, which wasn't cheap at all. Ten percent was all she could afford most months. However, she was hopeful things would change soon when she finally made homicide detective and had the chance to get murderers off the street. *Real* murderers, like the one who'd killed her family.

A cacophony of emotions stirred inside her—rage fighting against fear and sadness—but none reached the podium. She hated feeling out of control when facing a terrible situation she couldn't do anything about. Kate forced herself to take a deep breath and see the silver lining to this dark cloud. At least her uncle would be getting three square meals a day for free.

"Most of the court-appointed lawyers are good," she said.

"Be honest with him. Tell him everything you can. It has to be a mistake. Did they say anything else?"

Kenny shrugged again and shook his head. "They found my blood and my DNA at the crime scene."

"What?" Kate couldn't comprehend how his genes could have made it there without him. "Did they say where the murder occurred?"

"No, but they asked if I had a car or access to one. He must live somewhere far from me."

"When was the last time you drove?"

"I told them. About thirteen years ago. I sold the car to cover some of Lucy's medical bills. I haven't driven since, not even a rental car. Remember your graduation from the police academy? I took the bus then a cab to get there. Made it in the nick of time."

Kate smiled and kissed him on the forehead. She remembered how much perspiration had been on his shirt that day. He must have run a lot as well after getting out of that cab. He had worn his best outfit: a short-sleeved beige shirt with vertical brown lines, a matching pair of brown pants, and a wide orange tie. But she also clearly remembered the smile on his face when he finally snuck his way to the family section of the reserved seats just as the guest of honor was delivering his speech. Kenny had been so proud of her.

He leaned toward her, his bony hands grabbing hers, and he said, "I'm not perfect, but I'm no murderer. I don't want to die with this label added to the Murphy name. Our lineage has had enough of a bad rap. I still want to take you to Ireland before I die, you know? You need to see the Irish coast for yourself, see how green it is, how beautifully rugged the scenery is. You have to meet your cousins. Our family is bigger than you think. You'd love it there in Cork."

They sat still, hanging onto each other's hands as Kate let their physical bond temper the harsh reality.

The sound of a key in the lock brought her back to the here and now.

"Time's up," Reynolds said.

Kate gave Kenny one last hug and looked at him, "I love you. I'll do everything I can to make this right and get you out, okay? Just be brave and patient, and we'll fix this."

He squeezed her hands, nodded, and, for the first time in the fifteen minutes she'd spent with him, she saw hope appear in her uncle's teary eyes. She had to turn away before her own started to water.

After making her way back from the cells, she grabbed her things from the front desk and then headed home.

KATE SAT ALONE in her apartment, realizing there wasn't anything she could do until tomorrow. Nothing but hope that Capt. Cranston would tell her what was really going on and that their evidence wasn't airtight.

In the meantime, she occupied her mind by Googling the victim's name and found two articles that mentioned his death. There was no reference to her uncle... at least not yet. But chances were, his name would be in tomorrow's headlines.

She had to find a way to prove his innocence, and fast.

Purchase The Last Hope (second book in this series) here:
https://amazon.com/dp/B07C5CQ9ZG/

ABOUT THE AUTHOR

C.C. Jameson is an ex-military officer now wanderlust-driven author. Other than politically unstable countries, those with visa restrictions, or where only the wealthy can live, no place is out of bounds for the single, adventurous author.

At the time of publication, C.C. lived somewhere along the coast of Mexico, where blue skies meet turquoise waters, and cold beers and lime margaritas reign as the best thirst quenchers.

C.C. loves spending time alone in nature and writing at home. Hobbies include listening to live music, learning new languages, reading tons of books, and making up stories for readers to enjoy.

The name C.C. Jameson was born out of two authors' imaginations while chatting at a bar somewhere in Florida. Drinking was involved, of course, because it's one of C.C.'s favorite activities and a *must* for the introverted author while in social situations. As for the C.C. part, it corresponds to the author's real first initial, but doubled because it sounded better. Plus, that's how many people refer to *Canadian Club*.

So, C.C. Jameson is not just an anonymous author's pen name, it's a drinking name, too.

Learn more at http://ccjameson.com.

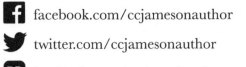

facebook.com/ccjamesonauthor

twitter.com/ccjamesonauthor

bookbub.com/authors/c-c-jameson

AUTHOR'S NOTES

Kate's story was inspired by what I've witnessed in the lives of friends and family around me.

I have female friends who've struggled with some of their male colleagues at work. I've heard my friends' first-hand tales, and I've seen the tears they cried years later when they relayed their stories. I've also seen the effects of domestic violence. (And I'm not just talking about physical beatings. Emotional abuse can arguably be worse.)

Perhaps this book is my way of coping with the information these brave women shared with me.

Bullying exists in almost every environment, and big, strong men aren't the only culprits; women are guilty of it, too. Abuse can come from anyone.

To better explain myself, I'll use the frog in the pot analogy, which you've probably heard before. If a frog jumps into a pot of boiling water, it will jump right out and return to safety. However, if the same frog is placed in a pot of lukewarm water that gradually gets heated up until it reaches boiling point, the frog won't jump out. It'll stay in and die.

I doubt anyone would choose a relationship with a violent, manipulative person. Like the frog, most would jump out: call it a bad date, delete the person's number, and then move on.

Violence and abuse often start slowly and gradually. The victim often doesn't realize it until much later. Excuses can often be made to explain the abuser's first small outbursts, which then become so regular that they redefine the norm. Things keep escalating from there, and the victim's tolerance and the number of false excuses made on behalf of the abuser also go up.

Until the final straw.

Perhaps it turns to physical violence (or not), but there's one point where the victim has a moment of clarity and realizes that she's no longer the person she used to be, she's had enough, and it's no longer acceptable for her to be treated the way her partner has been treating her. Her previous self would have never accepted it, but since the change was so gradual, it's as though it went unnoticed.

But along with this very important realization comes the biggest hurdle of all: the social pressure (perceived to be) imposed by those around the victim: *What will they think of me? I'm going to look so stupid. The whole neighborhood/company/family/etc. will see how weak I've been. They'll never forgive me for ruining my husband's reputation, tarnishing the family name, and/or destroying my kids' lives.*

Unfortunately, this is the stage where many victims get stuck, unable to leave because of … [fill in the blank with more excuses].

But I'm no psychologist. What I wrote above is based on my own experience, witnessing abuse from the outside. I'm grateful

I've never been a victim, but I can certainly understand how it could happen to anyone, including me.

I'll get off my soap box in a second, but I hope you're not the frog who's about to be boiled to death.

If you or someone you love is a victim of domestic violence or bullying, please get help. Lots of organizations exist at the municipal, state/provincial, and federal level in most countries.

Wikipedia provides several domestic violence hotlines, listed by countries:

https://en.wikipedia.org/wiki/List_of_domestic_violence_hotlines

https://www.stopbullying.gov/

https://ncadv.org/

If you suspect someone you love may be in an abusive relationship but don't know how to broach the topic, this fictitious story could be an option. Why not recommend this book to your friend?

Everyone deserves love and respect.

Don't be afraid to speak up.

ACKNOWLEDGMENTS

I would like to thank my editor, Claire, for helping me make the most out of this story. She's truly gifted at making words sing. I'd also like to thank Sébastien and Scott for answering my police questions. My friend Rachael has been wonderful with finding typos in various documents associated with my books. Thanks also to Graham who helped me fix a few things just before publication.

Thanks to all my friends and family for their encouragement and support. Thanks to my writer friends for their support and help with marketing this book.

Special dogs were immortalized in this story:

- **Rory**: a wonderful, happy, and sometimes stubborn corgi who wheels around his neighborhood thanks to the cart that his parents, Steph and Tony, built for him. I was lucky to spend a few weeks with him while his parents were traveling.

- **Carina**: a lovely Mexican street dog who's provided me with morning and evening cuddles for the past six months, since my roommate Jeannie moved in. Carina's fur is white and caramel, but otherwise she looks nothing like the dog I described in the book.
- **Yoda**: Although his name doesn't appear in the book, he's the dog I described as Carina (save for his gender, of course). My little papillon currently lives with one of my sisters and her son. He's adorable, even if he has little accidents in the house from time to time. I miss him greatly.
- **The Bobs**: My childhood best friend, Annie, lost both her Li'l Bob and Big Bob in recent years. Li'l Bob was a toy poodle not unlike the one who died during the race in my book (except Annie would never dare give any of her dogs a ridiculous name like the one I used). Li'l Bob was a smart and fun-loving little fellow who looked really cute in his John Deere cap. His brother, Big Bob, was a handsome Bernese mountain dog with a big heart and very soft fur. May they both rest in peace.

And **very special thanks to you, dear reader**. Without your support, I wouldn't be able to express the stories I want to share with the world. I'd probably drive myself crazy if I just kept my words spinning in my head.

Thank you for reading, for leaving a review, and for recommending my books to your friends.

You mean the world to me.